In Harm's Way

Allison crouched behind cover away from the cabin. I circled the cabin, finding nothing, then I went out behind the padlocked outbuilding and scanned the surrounding hills.

That's when I saw Nikki Scarborough. She was lying face down about twenty yards up the slope beyond the cabin. I went to her, but didn't touch the body. She had a small-caliber entry wound at the base of her skull. Blood trickled feebly from the wound into the ground next to her face. Her fingers dug into the ground on either side of her, as if she were trying to claw her way to safety.

"Bragg!" Allison called in warning.

I slid to the ground and brought up my .38 in a two-handed grip. The murderer was still in the vicinity, and Allison sensed it as well as I did.

But where was the killer now?

Also by Jack Lynch

SAUSALITO
SAN QUENTIN

Published by
WARNER BOOKS

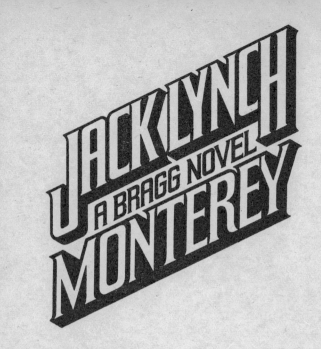

JACK LYNCH
A BRAGG NOVEL
MONTEREY

WARNER BOOKS

A Warner Communications Company

Chapter 1 ————————

It was the wrong girl at the wrong time, but she'd seen me and seemed to recognize me, and I couldn't ignore her. I hitched up my pants, went over to the pottery stall and said hello.

"It's been a long time," she said, but it was obvious she couldn't remember how long, or where or under what circumstances. But none of that mattered much. She was the girl I used to see from time to time—in the company of another man—during one of the most awful times of my life, when my marriage had broken down and I'd quit the newspaper job and was all at war with myself. She would come into the establishment on the arm of a man who was short and swarthy. She, in contrast, was tall and cool and willowy. She had a wide, Charlotte Rampling mouth and slate-gray eyes. Her voice was as calm and fine as the dark hair that fell to her shoulders. I had, in a way, fallen in love with her with the awful ache that accompanies a truly messed-up life. Back then I had badly needed somebody to hold my hand and tell me things would get better. Back then, on those lonely nights in my Sausalito apartment when I couldn't get to sleep, I would pretend that she was lying beside me telling me that things would get better and a couple of other things as well.

But she hadn't told me that back then, and she

didn't tell me that now. Instead, she searched my face, trying to remember.

"Did we meet in the Valley?"

She meant the Carmel Valley, since it was the one the people down here always meant, being just over the long hill from Monterey and back inland.

"No, more like at a bar in Sausalito a few years ago."

She grinned and remembered. I'd been the tall and brawny guy behind the bar who'd given her and her fellow a free drink from time to time, and would flirt with her softly when the short, swarthy fellow went back to the men's room. She had come from Bellingham, originally, a town eighty miles north of Seattle, and Seattle had been where I'd come from. It was a starting point. A common touchstone in the past. I had wanted to spend time with her very badly back then. But I knew her fellow, sort of, and that was enough to keep me from trying to move in on her, even though the fellow was married to another woman.

"God, that was forever ago," she told me. She reached out and touched my arm. Briefly.

She was wearing a light blue pants suit with a creamy colored, wide-brimmed hat. There was something about her eyes that let you know she'd walked down a couple of long roads since those days in Sausalito, but other than that she was as beautiful— no, more beautiful, wiser—than ever. The only problem with all this was that back inside the main arena of the Monterey County Fairgrounds, listening to the closing number of the Bobby Hutcherson Percussion Ensemble, was Allison France, the quiet blonde artist from Barracks Cove with whom I had—once— even tentatively discussed the hair-raising subject of marriage.

"I don't remember your name," she told me, more in astonishment than apology.

"Peter Bragg. And I never did know yours, other than Jo."

"I always regretted that," she told me evenly. Forthright, if nothing else, this girl. "The other name is Sommers, these days."

"It wasn't that when you were going with Jimmie John?"

"No. I've married since then." She turned to the thin, lank-haired girl running the pottery stall. "Nikki, this is Peter Bragg. He's one of the ones who got away, a long time ago."

Nikki was a serious-looking girl in a blue smock who could smile when something touched her right, and Jo's remark had done that.

"If I'd thought seriously she didn't want me to get away," I told Nikki, "I would have chained myself to a nearby tree."

"You two look good together," said Nikki, doing her part to further the mischief.

"Well," said Jo Sommers, with a very correct face, "what do you suppose we should do about that?"

"If your husband isn't around, we could go up to the Hunt Club and I could buy you a drink and we could stand around the bar and let everybody see how swell-looking we are together."

"I would like that," Jo told me, giving me a stare that went through my eyes and out the back of my head and part way across the Pacific Ocean.

"Hey, this isn't a dating service I run here," said Nikki. "Buy something."

I turned and looked at the display of glazed crockery and knickknacks. I picked out a maroon coffee mug that said "Monterey Jazz" on the side, along with the last two digits of the year. "I'd buy this, but

I don't want to haul it around for the rest of the evening."

"Pay now and pick it up when you're ready to leave," said Nikki, taking the mug and wrapping it in newspaper.

I paid. Jo Sommers took my arm and we walked up the grassy fairway, past other stalls selling posters and T-shirts, straw hats and dreams.

"Did you marry well?" I asked her.

"I married comfortably. And you?"

"I never married again, if that's what you mean."

"That's what I mean. I recall now that Jimmie John said you'd recently split up with your old lady back then, in Sausalito. You were quite miserable."

"Jimmie John said I was miserable?"

"No, I could tell that for myself, although you put on a very good front."

"Well, that was a long time ago," I reminded her. "At least I've got a girl now, a good one. A lady who paints things, and is starting to make a name for herself among the art crowd, on the West Coast, at least. She's inside listening to the music."

"Why is she inside listening to the music while you're out roaming around buying drinks for other women?"

"She's a fan of the Latin singer coming on next. I'm not."

"Is she pretty? The girl friend, not the singer."

"She's very pretty."

Jo drew back her head and gave me a saucy look. "As pretty as I am?"

"Different. I wouldn't know how to compare the two of you. You're both startling and powerfully attractive, but in different ways. For instance, Allison is also deeply into carpentry. Built herself a studio out behind where she lives. Likes to hammer and saw and things like that. Know many other dames like that?"

"Goodness, no. That all takes so much muscle. I'd best watch my step around Lady Allison."

She said that last with the evil grin I used to think about during those lonely nights in my Sausalito apartment. And she also put the sort of move on me that would arouse the pagan in any man. As she said, "Lady Allison," she shifted the arm looped through my own and grasped my hand to press the back of it against one of her small, neat breasts, only for the time it takes to blink an eye, but unmistakable, provocative.

The Hunt Club was one of those semi-exclusive institutions that all communities seem to set up and treasure. For 362 days of the year it is just a middling-sized bar set up in the front of the building that houses the fairgrounds stage. For the three-day weekend of the Monterey Jazz Festival in September, though, it is exclusive turf, with admission by pass only. It was meant to be a restricted enclave where performers could relax before or after their performing, and media people could have access to them for interviews and such. If you had a pass to the Hunt Club, you were sort of a hotshot for the weekend. The scrambling to get one of those could get close to nasty. I happened to have one because I had a friend on the *Monterey Herald*, Billy Carpenter, who also was one of the founding organizers of the festival and a member of the board of directors. Billy was quietly proud of his role in making the festival a reality.

"It integrated Monterey," he told me one time, meaning not only the city of Monterey, but the next-door communities of Carmel and Pacific Grove as well. In 1958, the first year the festival was staged, in an attempt to prolong tourist traffic at the start of the off season, it was said that many of the hotels and motels in the area wouldn't take reservations over the phone from anybody with a Southern accent. That has changed.

The private security guard at the door to the Hunt Club barely glanced at my pass. I think he remembered me from the year before. There was a lively crowd inside. There always is. Laughter and chatter echoed off bare walls. There's not much pretension about the Hunt Club. It's a plain sort of place where a fellow can pop in and get a quick drink during the horse shows and other exhibitions they hold during the year at the fairgrounds. An open lounge area just inside the door was outfitted with very utilitarian tables and chairs. In one corner was a large television projector suspended from the ceiling. During the jazz festival, a closed circuit TV system showed the performance on stage. The backstage area itself was just beyond the back of the lounge area. Photographers wander through from time to time to take advantage of small, round viewing ports cut through the stage backdrop.

"Let's go to the bar," I told Jo. "There's an open stool there if you want to sit."

"Fine."

We made our way past people. Jo asked for a snifter of brandy. I had a bourbon and water. We touched glasses, and she gave me what I took to be a conspiratorial look.

"Have any children?" I asked in straight-arrow fashion.

She wrinkled her nose. "No. Do you? That you know of?"

"No. Is back in the Valley where you live?"

She shook her head. "But my husband and I attend quite a few social functions in there. And there's the tennis ranch. We live on the hill just south of the artichoke fields along the Carmel River. Carmel Highlands, it's called."

"I know. Expensive area. You married well."

"I married late."

"What does your husband do?"

"He's retired."

"Military man?"

"He was, once. What do you do these days?"

I gave her a business card and looked away. She let out a hoot. "Honest to God? A private eye?"

"Something like that."

She was looking at me with, if anything, an even more mischievous look than before. "Is it perilous and exciting?"

"Any job that has you dealing with people in California these days can be perilous and exciting."

"Do you carry a gun?"

"Sometimes."

"Show me."

"Now isn't one of the times. I promised my girl friend that this weekend would be just for the fun of it. No work."

She reached out and squeezed my thigh. "I envy your girl friend." The squeeze lingered.

"You seem restless," I told her.

The smile went away, but her stare was very direct. "Yes, Peter. That's exactly what I am. Restless."

There was laughter and men's raucous voices behind me as a new group of people moved into the bar area. I felt a hand on my shoulder and turned. It was Billy Carpenter, my short, stocky friend from the *Monterey Herald,* wearing a red blazer the festival officials were sporting that year, along with the silver-gray golf caps they'd blossomed out in on the festival's twenty-fifth anniversary. He was smoking a cigar and standing with a group of similarly attired men.

"How's it going, Pete? Hello, Mrs. Sommers."

He briefly doffed the cap. Jo returned the greeting. She also knew some of the other men in the party. In turn, Billy introduced me to them. A tall, spindly fellow named Gus Wakefield; a smaller man named Whitey something; a short, thickly built gent with a gray crewcut named Pitt; and another man whose name I didn't catch. None of them would see the lower side of fifty again, and they all drank Scotch.

"Doc around?" Billy asked.

"No, he doesn't like this sort of music," Jo told him. "He's home, probably listening to Brahms and reading Nietzsche."

Billy Carpenter assumed a shudder. "That's pretty obscure stuff."

"That's my husband," said Jo.

"I have to go to the head," said Whitey.

"Doc?" I asked Jo. "Your husband's a physician?"

"A shrink," she told me.

"What's your boyfriend do?" asked Wakefield, with a broad enough smile for me so I didn't have to take offense.

"Careful, Gus," Jo told him. "He's a private dick from San Francisco. I knew him when he was a bartender."

"Why would anybody quit a swell job like tending bar to become a private cop?" asked the fellow whose name I hadn't caught. None of this bothered me. They were all a little drunk, obviously unwinding after getting another jazz festival under way.

"Seriously," the fellow continued. "Seems to me a bartender with your rugged appearance would have a social life to make the rest of us howl with envy."

"You do meet a lot of people," I admitted, "but there comes a point where you feel it's time to move along."

"I wouldn't," he assured me, turning to catch the

eye of a bartender and making a circular motion over his head to buy a round of drinks for all of us.

Things went along in this disjointed manner, pretty much ending the conversation I'd been having with Jo Sommers. Just as well, I felt. It had gone a bit further than it should have anyway, with Allison sitting out in the arena.

On the TV monitor I watched Jimmy Lyons, the main honcho of the Monterey Jazz Festival since its inception, come onto the stage applauding politely, trying to indicate to the female Latin vocalist it was time to move along to the next act. The female vocalist ignored him and swung into yet another dizzy tune. Lyons withdrew gracefully. Personally, I would have put a come-along hold on her and dragged her off into the wings.

"I'm going to have to wander back into the arena or my lady will begin to wonder what became of me," I told Jo. I was half turned away from the gentlemen again, facing Jo Sommers on her stool. She gave me a pouty expression.

"Do you have to? It's been so long."

When she said this she put her hand out to squeeze my leg again. Up high. She relaxed the hand but left it there and then let it drift some. Things were crowded and busy enough around us so that anybody not right there on his hands and knees wouldn't have noticed, but this wasn't the sort of trouble I needed right then. I shifted my position to disengage whatever she was up to.

"I have to. Maybe another time," I told her.

"Maybe we'll see each other again during the weekend," she said.

"Maybe," I agreed. "But I'm apt to have Allison with me next time."

"Your idea, or hers?"

"Probably mine. I'm the sort of guy who can only

concentrate on one girl at a time. Can't handle the complications that crop up, otherwise."

"I thrive on them," she told me.

But at least she let me get out of there without any more fondling. I decided the marriage with the doctor must be dull.

Chapter 2

The town of Carmel is on the western slopes of a tall hill that plunges down to the edge of the Pacific Ocean. It has a population of five thousand and was said to have been named by Sebastián Vizcaíno in honor of some Carmelite monks traveling with him and his band of explorers who camped near the Carmel River in 1602. But the town didn't really get on its feet until about 170 years later when Padre Junípero Serra relocated his mission near the same river. He'd moved it from what was described as the rowdy influences of the growing town of Monterey, up north. Probably the reason Monterey had been getting too rowdy for a proper Christian environment was that it has a fine harbor. If you've ever lived in a seaport town and seen the sailors and others that type of town draws, then you'll appreciate why Padre Serra picked up his priestly skirts and moved south. Monterey went on to become a Spanish military post and after that a whaling port. The canneries and John Steinbeck came later.

Due west of Monterey, at the northern tip of the Monterey Peninsula, is a town called Pacific Grove. Pacific Grove is noted for two things, the annual November fly-in of thousands of monarch butterflies from Alaska and other points north, and its historic reputation as California's last dry city. They hadn't allowed spirits proper into the town's retail establishments until 1969. But then, it was only a short drive east to Monterey, or south to Carmel.

Between Pacific Grove and Carmel is the Del Monte Forest, which is part forest but also an exclusive residential community with some of the most scenically breathtaking golf courses in the world. Pebble Beach, Cypress Point and Spyglass Hill are all there, laid out alongside the Pacific. The Bing Crosby Pro-Am Golf Tournament is held on those courses every year in late January or early February. Some of the nation's finest professional golfers are paired up with members of the smart set from Hollywood, various athletes and assorted industrialists to drive off the tee into howling gale-force winds and putt across rain-soaked greens.

Carmel used to be a hangout for writers and artists, but then it became a trendy place to visit, driving up real estate prices and for the most part forcing out the creative people. The Spanish mission at the south end of town set the tone for Carmel's low, stucco, Spanish style of architecture in the business district, while its groves of cypress and pine trees seemed to set the residential pattern of tucked-away cottages. Hansel and Gretel and the witch would have felt right at home in Carmel.

Among the shops catering to the tourist trade are several dozen art galleries. I was standing in one of them in a shopping square called Carmel Plaza, in the heart of town. Allison France was at the other end of the plaza casing the fine clothing in the I. Magnin store. Why, I couldn't say. About the only thing I'd ever seen her wear, though she wore them well, were jeans and shirts designed for men.

The art gallery I was in specialized in Western art. Cowboys and Indians and frontier soldiers and grizzly bears. It's my kind of stuff. I had family who'd taken part in all that. On a lower level and at the other end of the plaza was a crackerjack bookstore that had the largest collection of war literature, fact and fiction, I'd ever come across. It took me a couple of visits to figure out that probably the reason for that was the large retired military community in the area. I'd never found out why so many former generals and admirals and officers of lesser rank chose to retire in the area. Fort Ord, home of the 7th Infantry Division, was a few miles up the road north; and not far from the fairgrounds in Monterey was the Navy Postgraduate School. Maybe people passing through those posts liked what they saw and decided to come back. Or maybe it was all those golf courses.

The painting I'd been staring at for a few minutes wasn't about frontier soldiers. It showed two men on horses, one of them leading a laden jackass. They were in a wooded thicket, racing hell-bent through the field of vision alongside a stream. The men were in buckskins. They had intense, driven expressions on their faces. One of them was looking over his shoulder.

I was strongly drawn to those two men, their three animals and whatever it was they were hoping to escape from. I felt as if a part of me might have been included in that particular scenario. Either running from, pursuing or lying in wait down the trail. Whatever.

"Who do you suppose is after them?"

I turned. Allison France stood at my shoulder. Five feet, eight inches of firm, trim, well-conditioned sinew and flesh; intelligent blue eyes; honey-blonde hair down past her shoulder blades. Heart's-desire kind of stuff. She was wearing jeans and a jazz festival T-shirt.

"I don't know. Indians, probably. A bear, maybe."

"Maybe the sheriff's after them. Can't tell what they might have in those saddlebags."

"That's true. Or maybe there is a Bigfoot and he's loping along after them."

"I doubt that. I'll stick with the sheriff."

"I'll put my money on the Indians."

"Why?"

"They killed a relative of mine."

"Oh? Who dat?"

"George Armstrong Custer."

She drew back with a small but genuine look of astonishment. "You serious?"

"Yup. Custer was my grandmother's maiden name."

"Do you always do Gary Cooper when you talk about General Custer?"

"Most of the time." I turned back to the painting. "I am really drawn to this thing."

Allison tilted her head and looked at a small blue price sticker on an edge of the frame. She gave me a look. "Twelve hundred dollars worth?"

"No. I'm not hardly attracted to anything that much. Did you find any rags you liked up at I. Magnin?"

"Lots, but none I can't get along without just now."

"Back to the thrift shop, hey?"

"What's wrong with that?"

"With your figure, nothing. You'd look good in swaddling clothes."

"Perhaps. Show me where you buy your clothes."

"What?"

"You told me one time you buy your clothes in Carmel. I'd like to have a look at the shop. Show me."

"I told you I bought *some* of my clothes in the area. It's not in town here, but back in the Valley six or eight miles. It's a small place that sells Western jeans and belt buckles and cowboy hats."

"What do you buy there?"

"Pants, mostly. That's where people from the ranches back in there buy their riding gear."

"Ever buy anything besides pants there?"

"Once."

"What?"

"A hat."

Her eyes grew a little wide. "A cowboy hat?"

"Yup. Has a dark blue denim sort of nap to it."

"I've never seen you wear a cowboy hat."

"Nobody's ever seen me wear a cowboy hat. Only time I wear it's when I'm home alone in my apartment."

"That's not fair. Why don't you ever wear it out where we can all see it? There are any number of us who'd just love to see you in your cowboy hat, Bragg."

"I suppose there are. But I have my clients to think about. Past and potential. I have a feeling it might cut into my business to the point where I'd have to go back to tending bar."

"I'd almost prefer that you did, if it weren't for the girls you'd meet, like the one you described to me last night."

"I didn't meet too many like her. And I never met even one like you. Took being a detective to get me up to Barracks Cove and meet a snazzy dame like yourself."

I got her. She couldn't think of anything to say and just sighed a little raggedly. We'd taken the outdoor escalator back down to ground level of the plaza and were looking in shop windows here and there when I saw a newspaper rack with that morning's *Monterey Herald*. I froze. Allison turned to stare at me.

"What is it?"

"That's her," I said, staring at the front page of the *Herald*. "The girl I met last night."

It was a picture of Jo Sommers, eyes downcast,

being led somewhere by an official-looking gent in civvies. The headline over the photo, and the caption beneath, told me that Jo's husband, the psychiatrist, had been murdered, and Jo was being held as chief suspect.

Chapter 3 ———————————

The sheriff's office wasn't telling the press a great
deal about what was supposed to have gone on at the
Sommers home the night before. The cause of death
was tentatively listed as suffocation, but the suffocat-
ing instrument wasn't identified. The person who
called for help was the victim's wife, Jo. And the rest
of it was pretty thin gruel, which wasn't surprising,
considering the state that relations between the press
and the government seemed to be reaching. Not that
cops and sheriff's deputies in Monterey County were
any worse than those in other places. It was a natural
outgrowth of the stance being taken in the nation's
capital, about what is proper for the citizenry to be
let in on. And this was the nub of it, so far as people
in the news-gathering business were concerned. They
were, after all, representing the public. When something of interest occurs, it is the business of the
ladies and gentlemen with notepads and Nikons and
those with minicams and microphones, to go to the
scene of the event and ask questions as representa-
tives of the public. You and I, sitting in our living
rooms, hear tell of an event, and there are quite
normal questions which pop to mind. How could
that have happened? Who did what? Why were those
people there? Who was in charge? Or even more
intriguing, who was the person who made that decision,

and upon what set of logic or ethics did he or she make it?

Edward R. Murrow, who was my un-met guru during my news-gathering days, set his sights on that last one time when he said that news used to be a fire engine going down the street—today it was what was going on in a given person's mind.

And that is what recent administrations in Washington wanted ever more increasingly these days to not disclose. And that official stance had been around long enough now to permeate every level of government. What it came down to was a bottom-line stance that it no longer is the people's right to know what is going on. Which, of course, is quite a ways removed from what they teach you in journalism school.

The story in the *Monterey Herald* did go on to say that Dr. Haywood Sommers was a nationally recognized psychiatrist who had specialized in military psychoses. Until right then I hadn't realized that there was such a specialization. But on second thought, it must have been a whale of a field. No wonder the Sommers could afford to live in Carmel Highlands. I offered the paper to Allison, so she could read about the death of the late Dr. Sommers, if she liked.

"No thanks. Not my line of work."

"Not mine, either. Not this weekend, anyhow."

"That's nice to hear," she told me.

In the past, we'd had a few other holidays and weekends that we'd planned to spend together abruptly interrupted by my work. More than a few. But then, that was the nature of the work. Trouble doesn't pick a convenient time to fall on somebody. So the somebody with the trouble doesn't always wait until a convenient time to come and offer to pay me for my time and services.

"It's probably just a mistake anyhow," I told her, sailing the *Monterey Herald* into a litter can.

"Probably," said Allison, putting her arm through mine and leading me on to the next shop window.

We looked into a lot of windows after that and even left the streets to go into the shops themselves from time to time. Allison remarked that the town was like one big toy department for adults. They sold shoes and clothing, kitchenware and wine, paintings and photos, leather goods and brass and several thousand other things, including items to slake a person's hunger and thirst.

Of course, after reading the newspaper story, my mind wasn't that much into the shops of Carmel. It more or less stayed on Jo Sommers and whether or not I thought she was capable of killing somebody. But that's not quite accurate either. I'm one of those people who believe that anybody, under certain circumstances, can be brought to take another human's life, if only to save their own neck or the life of another. But what I wondered about Jo was whether she was capable of killing somebody under other than these most extreme circumstances. The newspaper story hadn't said anything about the death's occurring in the middle of a heated battle between Jo and the doctor. And it didn't say anything about anybody else's being around in whose defense Jo might have battled to the death.

What I finally decided, drifting from shop to shop, ever more distracted, was that Jo was a dangerous woman, but not killing-dangerous. She could bewitch you in a number of ways, and she probably could screw up your life to the point where a man might be brought to consider suicide, but Jo wouldn't be caught doing the dirty act herself. If anything, I think she was a little afraid of violence. Still, as those things sometimes go, she also was a little bit fascinated by it. I think that is why she went with Jimmy John all those years ago. Jimmy John was quick with

his fists, as we used to say when I was growing up in
Seattle. And I recalled a time at the No Name bar in
Sausalito, when I worked there. It was one of those
rare occasions when Jo and Jimmy John came in
during the evening, and that particular night another rare event, for the No Name, occurred. Two
men near the front of the house started a slugfest.
Another bartender and I went over the top of the
bar and wrestled the combatants outside while Patty
the cocktail waitress held open the front door. When
the other bartender and I turned to go back inside,
one of the fighters stepped away from his opponent
and took a swing at me. I leveled him there on the
sidewalk. Jo Sommers, just inside the front door,
had seen it. If ever a woman had flashing eyes, that's
what hers were when I went back inside the bar. And
it was from that time on that we used to flirt softly
whenever Jimmy John went to the men's room.

Allison and I drove back out to the county fairgrounds early in the afternoon and walked up the
long, grassy promenade toward the Hunt Club building and main arena. Mark Naftalin and the Robert
Cray Band and some other people were performing
at the afternoon concert. I am not all that great a fan
of bluegrass and country music, but Allison is. And
there always was the added attraction of fan madness,
mostly female fan madness, during the Saturday and
Sunday afternoon concerts. Various young women
become so transported by the music booming through
the banks of loudspeakers on either side of the stage
that they get out of their seats and boogie in the
aisles. They sometimes are an erotic and far more
entertaining show than the fellows up there on the
stage plucking and tooting for pay.

But as we passed the stalls of pottery and posters
and jewelry and clothing, on our way to the arena
entrance, my mind still was on Jo Sommers, who

probably wouldn't boogie in the aisles but could be pretty erotic in her own fashion and was said by Monterey County authorities to have maybe murdered her psychiatrist husband. We were just outside the arena turnstiles when Allison stopped, swung around to face me and looped her long, tanned arms around my neck.

"Okay, Bragg, go see her."

"What?"

She gave me a look that told me I was underestimating her intelligence again. That is something I've never done with her, though. In fact, while I might know a thing or two she doesn't, when it comes to sheer smarts, I think she has it all over me.

"Ever since you read the story about your girl friend, it's like I've been walking around with a gent who has his mind on last year's regrets."

"She was never my girl friend."

"Okay, she was never your girl friend. But go see her. And give her a message from me."

"What message?"

"Tell her I wanted you to go hear her story, but that you're not to do anything about it until after this weekend. During the jazz festival, you're mine. That's the agreement we made, right?"

"Right."

"So go see her. But leave me your pass to the Hunt Club."

"What do you want that for? The place is the sort of dive where musicians and press people are apt to put the hit on you."

She gave me a little-girl smile I'd never seen before. I gave her a kiss and the pass to the Hunt Club and headed back for the exit gate.

The Monterey County Jail is about fifteen miles east of the fairgrounds, in Salinas, on Natividad Road. When the matron brought Jo into the interview room, she was wearing a blue jumpsuit—the jailhouse togs all the women prisoners wore that year. Jo gave me a tiny smile and sat across the table from me with a package of Newport menthol cigarettes and a book of matches in her hand. She took out a cigarette. I reached across the table and took the book of matches from her and lit her cigarette. She blew out a wisp of smoke with a little nod of thanks and leaned back in her chair to study me. She hadn't had a lot of sleep and she looked a little depressed, but she still was in good control of herself. She didn't have the god-awful desperate look that many did the first time they were put behind steel bars.

"What's this all about?" she asked.

"I'm here under orders."

"Whose orders?"

"Lady Allison. She noticed I became a little preoccupied after I read about your arrest."

Jo's right foot was arched on its toes, and she swung her knee back and forth, as if there was gritty tension built up in her. She was a woman, I decided, who would exude great sensuality even when sitting in a gas chamber.

"Why should you become preoccupied after reading about my arrest?"

I took a deeper than normal breath and let it out and stared at her a moment. "They aren't going to give us enough time together so we can flirt back and forth the way we used to up at the No Name when your fellow went to the can."

"Is that what we did back then?" She shook her head, regretting it as soon as she'd said it. "I'm sorry. I guess it's beginning to get to me, being in here. I'm glad you came. I can use all the help I can get. Thank your lady for me."

"I will. But she wanted me to give you a message,

which basically is that I'm to listen to your story, but not to do anything about it until after the jazz festival. I've disappointed her a lot in the past. I really can't do that again, this time."

"That's plenty fair enough. Thank her again."

"Monday, I'll start doing whatever I can to help you."

"I'd like that. Are you good at what you do?"

I hesitated a moment. "There are a lot of people I've worked for in recent years who would tell you I am. But I'm not infallible. I can be duped, and I can be dropped by a bullet, the same as any other man."

"You've been shot at?"

"More times than I like to think about. And I've got the scars to prove not everybody who shot at me missed."

"You'll have to let me see them sometime," she said with another little smile.

"Forget you're the vamp of Northern California and tell me what happened."

"Last night?"

"Yes. Did you kill him?"

"God, no. I'm not tough enough for that. My body is very good for some things, but not that. And my mind isn't tough like that, either. I rather think the closest I could come to being involved in death would have been back in old Roman times, if I were one of the pampered women in Caesar's box at the Colosseum, looking on at a victorious gladiator standing over another, sword poised, eyes searching out the royal box to see if the vanquished should live or die. I think I could quite easily signal thumbs-down, just for the excitement of watching a life taken."

I stared at her a moment. For the first time since I'd met her, the attraction I felt for her cooled off some.

"When did you get home?"

"Not too long after I saw you. Around eleven, I think. I was going to go back into the concert again, but I felt tired all of a sudden. I think seeing you took a lot of energy out of me. I have no idea why. It isn't as if we had experienced any consuming affair in the past. The possibility of it in the future, perhaps."

She shook her head and took a draw on the cigarette, then plucked a tobacco shred from her lip. "No matter. I just decided to say good night to Nikki and head back home. The lights were on when I got there. I heard the television in Woody's study. Everything seemed normal, but he didn't reply when I called out to him."

"Woody being your husband?"

"That's right. Haywood, actually. But I and a few privileged friends were allowed to call him Woody."

"What did you do when he didn't answer?"

"I went into the study. He was in his easy chair in front of the TV set. His head was on his chest, as if he'd fallen asleep. There was nearly a full drink of Scotch on the stand beside him. He's done that before, fallen asleep during a late show. I would rouse him and we would go into our beds."

"You slept separately?"

"Separate bedrooms, even. Why are you interested in that?"

I shrugged. I didn't really know why I had asked it.

"Anyway," she continued, "this time when I tried to rouse him he tumbled out of the chair onto the floor."

A little tremor fluttered her shoulders. "I was quite frightened at that. I had no idea what might be the matter. I knelt on the carpet and rolled him onto his back and tried again to waken him. When that failed I called an ambulance." She put out her cigarette and stared at the tabletop in front of her.

"What did you do while waiting for the ambulance?"

"I tried to make him comfortable." She looked up at me with a stark expression. "I didn't know he was dead. I thought people—when they were dead, I thought their bodies turned cold. His wasn't. He felt normal. I propped a pillow beneath his head. He was wearing a sweater over his shirt and tie. I loosened the tie and opened a button or two on the shirt so he might breathe easier."

She squeezed shut her eyes and dropped her head briefly. "I was doing this to a *dead* man," she said softly. "But I didn't know."

She shook her head and got another Newport out of the wrinkled pack. I reached for the matches, but she motioned my hand away and lit it herself.

"I was still fussing over him when the ambulance arrived, and a few minutes after that a deputy sheriff showed up. The ambulance people must have notified the sheriff's office something was wrong out at our place. It must have been a slow night; an officer responded."

She took a long draw on the cigarette and leaned back in her chair and stared at the ceiling. "Things went very badly after that. The ambulance attendants made a cursory examination of Woody. They wouldn't tell me what was wrong with him. They spoke quietly to each other a moment, then one of them said something to the deputy, and he in turn asked me to wait in an adjoining room. I was angry, because they wouldn't tell me what was wrong with Woody. But the officer was quite firm with me. I could sense a certain hostility." She lifted a shoulder and let it fall. "I went out to the kitchen and fixed myself a good stiff drink. That's what made the rest worse, I suppose. Some other men arrived soon after. They began doing the things I've read about them doing when there's been a death. Photos. Measuring things. I suddenly realized that my husband must have been dead. I went a little crazy then. I began screaming at them. Ordered them out of my house. I tried to get to Woody. I wanted to hold him. I thought it might help somehow. But they wouldn't let me near him. They finally put handcuffs on me, not very gently, either. I was mad. I was mad at all the strangers in my home, and I was mad at Woody for—for being dead like that. Two of them, detectives, I suppose, tried to talk to me. I wasn't a very cooperative witness. I was starting to go to pieces."

She ground out the cigarette and shook her head. She seemed near tears. "I cursed them. Soundly. My entire world was falling to pieces around me. I kicked out at them. I screamed. It wasn't really them I was mad at any longer. It was just, the things that had happened. I still didn't understand it all. I didn't understand what the deputies were there for in the first place, if Woody had had a heart attack or a stroke or whatever. But I was fighting back the only way I knew how. And that didn't help matters at all, of course. And by the time it was all over with, they brought me here."

"What was supposed to have happened to your husband?"

"They say somebody—me—smothered him, with the pillow I'd placed beneath his head. They found nasal hairs on it. Can you imagine such a thing?"

"Who told you this?"

"One of the detectives. The one who read me my so-called rights, then tried to get me to confess to killing my husband." She leaned forward, her hand on the table balled into a fist.

"Well, let me tell you. It is a very routine and dull thing on a television show or in a movie when the police read a suspect his rights. But last night, I listened. When they read that statement to me off a little card, I listened like I've never listened in my life. And I didn't tell them anything. And I told them I wouldn't be telling them anything until my lawyer was sitting at my side."

"Good for you."

She nodded and leaned back in her chair. And then she began to cry. She was quiet at first. A little shudder went through the upper part of her body, and then a small animal sound leaped out of her throat. She leaned forward until her head was on the table, while a long keening noise came from her and one of her hands beat softly on the table top.

It was a couple of minutes before it passed. I handed a fresh handkerchief to her. She composed herself, finally, and lit another cigarette.

"You must have loved him more than you've let on."

She looked at me sharply. "I didn't," she snapped, "but I didn't want the son of a bitch to die on me, either."

Chapter 4

I asked Jo if there was anything I could get her. She shook her head.

"They don't let us have anything from outside. You could be a dear and go by home and feed the cat. It's a Siamese blue point. Her name is Sam."

She gave me the address and told me where she kept a spare key for when she or her late husband locked themselves out. She said it was on a nail driven into the inner side of a piece of timber supporting their hot tub in the back patio.

Then her mind took an abrupt, kinky turn. She was fingering the material of the jail jumpsuit. "It's too bad they won't let a person wear their own clothes in here," she said. "I'd love for you to be able to bring me back some underthings."

Then she set about describing the underthings she wished I could bring her. She said she bought them at a boutique in Carmel that called itself the Dream Shop. She said it carried specialty wear, which she described in some detail, about how slick it felt caressing her body—I think that was the term she used—and how it certainly beat the sort of thing a girl could pick up at J. C. Penney's.

Then she wanted to tell me about some of the erotic fantasies she would have from time to time wearing these particular garments, but that was when

I told her it was high time for me to get back to the fairgrounds and collect Allison.

But driving back to the fairgrounds, I decided to swing by the Sommers home first and feed the dumb cat. Besides, I wanted a look at the scene of the crime.

What I found at the address Jo had given me was a rambling, single-story structure with brick exterior walls painted white and windows trimmed in gun-metal blue. Other people had gotten there ahead of me. It turned out I knew one of them. Two years earlier I'd been in the Monterey area working on a runaway case. A girl of about fourteen had become bored with life up in the Napa Valley and was last seen on the jumpseat of her seventeen-year-old boyfriend's motorcycle headed south. Her family hired me to get her back. I started out by contributing to the delinquency of any number of Napa Valley minors by buying a lot of beer for a weekend party, and in that way got on speaking terms with young people who knew the fourteen-year-old girl and her boyfriend. And that in turn led me down first to Big Sur, then back up to the Carmel area. The case had a mixed ending. The boyfriend ended up being stabbed to death at a beach near the artichoke fields along the Carmel River, and the girl was kidnapped by the people who had done the knifing. She did a lot of growing up in the next two days, until a Monterey County homicide investigator named Wally Hamlin and I tracked them down, and I got the girl and Wally got the killer of her late boyfriend. By the time it was all sorted out, the Napa Valley looked a little better to the girl, and Wally Hamlin and I were pretty good friends. And since Monterey County doesn't have all that many homicide investigators, it wasn't too much of a coincidence that Wally was in the Sommers home when I showed up and explained my interest in the latest killing and asked if he'd seen the cat named Sam.

He gave me a look and said no. "Whatever happened to that young girl you found down here last time?" he asked me.

"She went home and behaved herself for a couple of years, then got all edgy again and ran off and married some sailor she met in Vallejo," I told him.

Wally made a face and opened the door wider so I could go inside. "Makes you wonder why you're in the business sometimes, doesn't it?"

I agreed with him and stepped into a house that was occupied by people who obviously liked to live well. The interior gamely carried out the Carmel Spanish mission motif, although the Highlands were beyond the town limits of Carmel. The walls and ceilings were swirled in white plaster. The front room had large picture windows looking west, out over the shores of the Pacific, along with a couple of original Picassos that didn't make any sense at all to me. The red tile floor was covered with a fancy Chinese rug that had a royal blue background and small inset renditions of streams and glades and hoop bridges and sampans. The fireplace was stoked with logs all ready to be touched off, but it was so clean in there it didn't look as if anything had been fired up for about ten years. A couple of satsuma vases stood at attention at either end of the fireplace mantel, and a black leather sectional sofa and a couple of matching easy chairs were spotted about the room.

"Cheery," I remarked.

"Makes me feel like I should take off my shoes," said Wally. "The murder room's this way."

I followed him down a long hallway, our shoes whispering across more thick carpeting, this a rich burgundy color. Some more original paintings, not Picassos, but just as nutty, looked down on our journey.

The doctor's study had a lot of bookcases; an old, oak rolltop desk; a sofa and chair, TV set and stereo system. On the walls were the sort of valiant battle-action paintings depicting land, sea and sky you'd expect to find gracing the walls of the Pentagon. This room, too, had a small fireplace, and it looked well used. Overall, I estimated the size of the room to be about the same as the entire ground floor of the house I'd grown up in. We stood just inside the doorway. Wally watched me looking around.

"All this for one man to relax in?" I asked.

"Looks a little like the Fort Ord Officer's Club, doesn't it?"

I wandered over to the smaller fireplace mantel. No satsuma vases here, but there were several small plastic models, mostly military. There was a Boeing jet cargo plane, an intricate rendition of a water-cooled .50-caliber machine gun with its barrel pointed groundward, a model of a fighting ship with the numeral 35 on its prow, an army ambulance with Red Cross symbols on its sides and top, some sort of jet attack plane looking scorched and damaged and a miniature stockade that had human figures with hollow-eyed faces looking out through a mesh wire fence.

"What's this all about?" I asked.

Wally shrugged. "I didn't know the man, myself."

I crossed to the easy chair in front of the TV set. "This is where the body was."

"When we got here, the body was on the floor," Wally said.

"His wife told me he was in the chair when she found him. I have to take her version of things, or there's no reason for me to be here. Somebody held a pillow over his face?"

"Right."

"Probably from behind," I said, "if I go with her version. It would take somebody with muscle to do it without leaving signs of a struggle."

"Not necessarily," said Wally. "We won't have all the lab work done until sometime next week, but there were indications he'd been drinking like he knew it was his last night. And he'd taken a tranquilizer of some sort as well. If she'd just left him alone a while longer, he'd probably have snuffed himself."

"You think she did it, Wally?"

I turned to look at him. He was a short, beefy man with a red-veined nose and a scar on his jaw where a bullet had gone through it during the nation's Vietnamese pacification efforts.

"I don't know, Pete. The D.A. likes her for it."

"What sort of man is the D.A.?"

"Thackery? He's a hotdog. Ambitious. Wants to be governor someday. Maybe president. He's into building a solid conviction rate. Prosecutes some cases himself, which can be dicey for a politically ambitious man, but he has a staff that does good prep work."

"Why does he want Mrs. Sommers for this?"

"Two things, mainly. Our people got here literally minutes after the man died. If she didn't do it, she'd almost have to have been standing here watching while somebody else did it."

"She told me she found him that way, head lolling on his chest, when she got home from the jazz festival. I saw her there myself. We had a drink in the Hunt Club."

"Did she tell you about the fight?"

"What fight?"

"The one she had with her husband. It was all down on a little tape recorder sitting on his desk there."

"No, she didn't tell me about that. You figure the fight was last night?"

"She talks about going to the jazz festival on it. Yeah, we figure it was last night."

"What did they fight about?"

"Money. Her being tired of his crabbiness. His suspicions of her screwing around with other men. Usual stuff. Toward the end she talks about leaving him. For good. He tells her in turn to help herself. Says—if I remember it right—he's been thinking about throwing her trashy ass out onto the street for a long time anyhow."

"Why do people who feel that way about each other stay together, do you suppose?"

"Beats hell out of me."

"Could I listen to the tape?"

"I doubt it. The D.A.'s got it. He'll say no. Her lawyer will be able to, if they go to trial."

"She going to be charged?"

"Don't know. That's for Thackery to say. He'd like to. That's why I'm here again today, supposedly finding something more to nail her with."

"Have you?"

"Nope. But then, I'm a little more open-minded than Thackery. I'd like to find the killer, period. Mrs. Sommers, or the man next door or whoever. I've spent a couple of hours talking to neighbors. Nobody saw or heard anything unusual last night, before the ambulance arrived. Then I went around looking at windows and things for signs of a pry bar. Didn't find any. When we got here last night the patio door was closed and locked. Which would seem to mean whoever killed the man had a key or was let into the house by the victim himself. Mrs. Sommers had a key, of course."

"And there's a spare hanging on a nail on the hot tub platform out back in case they locked themselves out. That's how I was going to get in, if the coroner didn't have the place sealed."

Wally looked at me sharply. "Let's go see about that key."

We went out to the patio. I went to the side of the platform where Jo said they kept it. I squatted and searched the inside of the beams. Wally handed me a penlight, and a moment later I saw it.

"There." I pointed.

Wally got down beside me and nodded. He reached up and took hold of it by the notched shank and lifted it off the nail. He took it back inside, calling for the lab technician who'd accompanied him.

I climbed the short stairway to the hot tub deck. The water looked as clean as one would expect it to look, being a part of this particular house. Some sort of aerator or filter made a track of small bubbles rising from the bottom of the tub. The hum of an electric motor came from a nearby shed.

The patio was screened off from the rest of the backyard by laticework walls covered thickly with brilliant red bougainvillea blossoms. An arched gate in one corner opened into the fenced-in rear of the property. I went back down the stairs and through the gate to take a swing around the perimeter of the yard. One side of the house was bordered by a narrow strip of grass. Up toward the front was a warped wooden gate that squawked when I opened and closed it. The house was built up off the ground high enough so you wouldn't be able to see into the windows without using a stepladder. I retraced my steps to the rear of the house and went around to the other side. The property sloped down a sharp little bank on that side, to the tall wooden fence separating the Sommers place from the home next door. Ice plant covered the slope, making your footing a little treacherous. I walked on up alongside the garage to the driveway in front. The property dropped in neat terraces to the street. There was more ice plant and miniature shrubs and moss among little beds of white stone chips. Black wrought-iron railings guarded the concrete stairway to the street below. Off in the distance, gentle white combers came home to the beach. I looked around at neighboring houses. It seemed to be the sort of place where everybody stayed inside minding their own business.

Wally and the technician came out the front door.

"Find anything?" I asked.

"Good thumbprint," Wally told me. "But it's probably one of theirs. Whoever locked themselves out last. You staying?"

"If it's all right. I have to feed the cat."

Wally nodded. "We're through, so far as I can see. Thackery isn't going to be happy with what we have to tell him. I think the lady's going to be coming home when her forty-eight hours is up."

We said good-bye, and they got into a car parked down on the street and drove off. Just before I turned and went back inside, I saw a small movement at the edge of a drape in a window across the street.

Inside I called for the cat while taking a quick peek at the other rooms in the place. The temptation was great to take more than a peek, to try to get a feel for the people who lived there. But the clock was running, and Allison, by now, would be wondering about me. So I paused only briefly in what looked like a sewing room, but with no evidence of a sewing machine, a couple of bathrooms and the two bedrooms. They all were spacious, but had about the same warmth as the hallway. The only room in the place that reflected a human personality was the study where the doctor's body had been found.

Out in a corner of the kitchen was a newspaper on the floor with a red plastic water dish on it, nearly empty. I filled it with fresh water, called Sam's name a few more times and poked around in cupboards until I found the stash of canned cat food. Another plastic dish was in a drain alongside the sink. I figured if anything would bring the cat it would be the sound of the electric can opener, and I was right. I had the lid off and was starting to dump the contents into the dish when a jungle yowl came from the doorway.

I had forgotten what a racket a Siamese can make, at mealtime, during mating season and whenever else it wanted to get your attention. In the confines of the kitchen it was deafening. The animal was rubbing its sleek, dark fur against one side of the doorway. As I finished emptying the can, she trotted across the floor and gave my ankle a massage. Those who bring food, even complete strangers, are welcome in the house of the cat. I put the dish down alongside the water bowl and Sam ate. I didn't know if the animal had an escape hatch to outdoors or if there was a box of kitty litter around, and I didn't take the time to find out. I left the house and zipped back over the hill, then took the Aguajito Road exit that led to the county fairgrounds.

By the time I found a parking place alongside the road at the south gates and got into the grounds themselves, people already were coming down the long grassy avenue from the arena. When I reached the community of food stalls and trailers near the Hunt Club, everybody else started spilling out, and I knew I'd missed the last of the afternoon concert. I didn't even bother going into the arena itself but headed for the bar. The guard at the door recognized me, and I went on inside and found Allison standing at the bar like one of the boys, carrying on a laughing conversation with some of the older ducks I'd seen with Billy Carpenter the night before when I'd stopped in with Jo Sommers. I made my way over to her. As I wedged into the bar she gave me a playful poke to the shoulder without missing a beat in the story she was telling. I ordered a double gin and tonic, and a moment later, after getting a big laugh with the punchline of the story she'd been telling, she turned to me.

"Double?"

"I figured from the looks of things I had some catching up to do. How was the concert?"

"Mr. Bo Diddley showed up, as advertised. What more needs saying?"

"Who's Bo Diddley?"

Her eyes rose to the ceiling then came back to me. "Anyway, it was quite a performance. Hands clapping in the seats, hips shaking in the aisles. I loved it, and I'm glad you brought me down here. How did it go with you?"

I started to tell her, but then noticed that while the tall gent she'd been talking to had turned slightly away, he wasn't talking to anybody else just then, and I suspected he was listening to us.

"I'll tell you about it later. Sorry I'm so late."

"Didn't matter. Mr. Wakefield here saw me sitting all alone and came down during one of the intermissions to invite me up to his box. Have you met Gus?"

With the mention of his name, the man she'd been talking to turned with a look of kindness. "I hope you don't mind, Mr. Bragg. I saw the two of you in here together after last night's concert, some time after Billy Carpenter first introduced us. I said to myself then, my lord, but what a circle of handsome women that man travels in. Then, when I saw Miss Allison alone down there in one of those hard folding chairs, I just had to invite her up to my seats in the stand for some Chardonnay and Brie."

The Miss Allison is what made something fall into place in my mind. The man had a whisper of the South in his speech.

"I don't mind," I told him. "It was thoughtful of you to invite her. How long do you have to be a season ticket holder before you get seats in the grandstands?"

"Oh, about twenty years, I imagine. Miss Allison told me you've been visiting with Mrs. Sommers, poor woman. How is she?"

"Holding up about as well as you can expect of a person sitting inside a jail cell."

"It was a terrible shock to us all. Dr. Sommers was well known in the community. Did Mrs. Sommers tell you what happened?"

"I didn't go into it all that much with her."

"I see. Well, maybe we'll have a chance to talk a little more about it tonight."

Allison had a small smile on her face. "Gus has invited us to a party he's having at his place tonight. Anytime after the first set at tonight's concert."

"Yes, it's for my wife, really. We ordinarily wouldn't do such a thing during the jazz festival, but it's our fortieth wedding anniversary. Billy Carpenter and some of the other fellows you met last night will be there as well. And even if you want to sit through all of tonight's concert, I suspect there'll be some whiskey left at the Wakefield house. Personally, I feel these performances run overly long on Saturday nights."

"It's kind of you to invite us," I told him. "I'm sure we'll be able to make it." I shifted my gaze. "Does Miss Allison here know how to find your place?"

"Gus was kind enough to draw me a little map," she said, batting her eyes for me.

A little more room had opened up behind me along the bar. I moved back and tugged Allison with me, then lowered my mouth to just alongside her ear.

"What say we get out of here. Go off together, somewhere. Just the two of us."

"What did you have in mind?" she asked in a guarded tone.

"There's a kind of nice motel I know about, over in Carmel, near the water. Has a great, whopping big bed and a bottle of gin inside a small refrigerator built into the cabinet beneath the color TV set."

She stood up, drained her glass and slapped one hand on the bartop. "Let's go, podner."

Chapter 5 —————————

The motel I'd booked us into was a collection of white-painted wooden cottages, some of them two-story, double units, scattered down a grassy slope a dozen blocks south of Carmel's main business district and a block up from the water. It was quiet and within easy walking distance of the squeaky white sand of Carmel Beach. South of the beach, a road ran past fine homes of individual character built just above the ocean. The seaward side of one structure resembled a ship's prow pointed toward the oncoming waves. Another had copper trimming along the eaves that had turned green in the sea air, just like the Statue of Liberty. These were showplace homes, with huge, airy rooms and lots of glass looking out over the aqua-green water and jagged rocks rising from the seabed and clumpy kelp beds where otters basked and played. I'd been told that one-time movie actress Jean Arthur lived in one of those homes, or at least used to. She'd been a favorite of mine when I was growing up in Seattle. Since coming to California, it had been an ongoing fantasy of mine that someday I would be walking down that oceanfront road in Carmel and Jean Arthur would be out pruning her Pride of Madeira hedge and I would pause and we would have a moment's chat, just so I could once again hear that fine, throaty voice that used to lift the hair on the back of my neck years ago in a darkened theater atop Phinney Ridge.

There were other places within easy walking distance of the motel that I wanted to show Allison, but I didn't know if I'd have the time, the way things were going. After we'd had some of the gin and tonic water we kept in the refrigerator under the television set, and done some of the romping around that seems like a lot more fun in a motel room than at home, it almost was time to grab a bite to eat and head for the fairgrounds again.

When I came out of the bathroom toweling off after a shower, I found Allison sitting in a trance at a window that looked out over the water and line of cypress trees across the street. We had the upper floor in one of the double-decker units. It had a grand view, and Allison was looking at it, sitting in something resembling a lotus position, wearing only a frayed gray sweatshirt with its sleeves cut off that she'd bought in her favorite thrift shop. Her elbows were propped on naked legs and her chin was cupped in her hands. She was squinting out to where the late afternoon sun was glaring off the Pacific. She had showered ahead of me, and I'd seen her sit down in that same chair before I went into the bathroom.

I put on a pair of gray flannel slacks and a white polo shirt, and brushed off the dark blue blazer I'd brought along from home. Allison still hadn't budged. I walked over and began to knead her neck and shoulders. She purred.

"Why don't you just take a picture," I suggested. "You can get a blowup and hang it on your bedroom wall. Look at it from time to time and remind yourself of these days of spirit and dazzle."

She finally sat up a little straighter and stretched her long arms. "You don't get it, Bragg. I want to draw what I see out this window, sometime."

"So draw it."

"The light's not right. And I don't have the right balance in mind yet."

"Balance?"

"What I have to get in. What has to be left out. There's just too much treasure for the eye out there. The trees and sea and sky. Angles and shadows. Glitzes of this and that I've never seen all put together like this even up in Barracks Cove."

"What's a glitz?"

"I don't know, just a word I use. But you know what I mean."

"I suppose I do."

"So, since it isn't the roof of the Sistine Chapel I have to work with, I have to figure out what to put in and what's got to stay out. That's always the challenge, but here more than most places."

I made another gin and tonic. She was still sitting at the window, her bare feet on the floor now, one hand on the windowsill and her shoulders partly turned, as if she were about to get up, but her mouth was puckered, and she continued to stare out at the scene in front of her. The sun was streaming through the window and seemed to heighten the shine to her honey-blonde hair until it almost hurt the eye to look at her.

"Would you marry me, if I asked you seriously sometime?" I asked.

"Probably not," she said, her eyes not wavering.

"Why not? Some girls would consider me a fair catch."

"Some would. Some girls would consider most anything a fair catch."

"Hey, not fair."

She turned then and came out of the chair. With a grin, she looped her hands around my neck, and stretched her neck and darted her tongue into one of my ears. I put down the gin and tonic and reached my hands beneath the sweatshirt to gently cup the pair of breasts from Barracks Cove which turned men's heads and made other women suck their lips in envy.

"Come off it, Bragg. You know it wouldn't work. We're a couple of independent roustabouts always insisting on having things go our own way."

"Not always."

"Most times," she said. "We live alone by choice. We set up our lives to avoid the knocks. We get selfish. People like you and me don't belong married to anybody."

"That's pretty harsh."

"I know, but it's true."

She kissed the tip of my nose and turned to go into the bathroom again and start doing things to her face. But at the doorway she turned back. "And then, there's always one other thing, Pete."

"What's that?"

"If we ever got married, or even lived together in sin, I just know there'd come a time when you'd do something that hurt me in a really bad way. You wouldn't do it intentionally, but it would happen, because of the nature of the beast that's you. You know what I mean. You did it once up in Barracks Cove, that first time we met. I don't think I could go through that again, emotionally. I think I'd take my own life, first."

Her face was in dead earnest. She went in and closed the bathroom door, and I sat down across from the blank television screen to think somber thoughts.

It was late by the time we got to Gus Wakefield's party. We'd been running late all night. We had dinner at a restaurant out on a long wooden pier at

Fisherman's Wharf in Monterey. It was a seafood house and we went there because Allison likes seafood. I don't, particularly. I would have had a steak, if there had been one on the menu, but there wasn't, so I settled for a seafood salad that had a lot of suspicious-looking blobs in it.

The evening concert at the fairgrounds started at a little after eight. We didn't get there until a bunch of guitar players were finishing the first set. Instead of going right in to the arena floor and the hard folding chairs awaiting us, we went into the Hunt Club and worked at getting a little buzz on. At least one thing Allison and I had in common—we work hard and we play hard.

A quintet came on next, which we listened to for a while over the closed circuit TV system, before deciding we should knock off the drinking or we wouldn't be able to find the car to get to Gus Wakefield's party .

"Maybe we should take a cab, anyhow," said Allison, her arm around my own as we made our way past the stalls.

Because of the party we were going to later, Allison was wearing a dress, a white linen number that showed off her bare, tanned legs to good advantage. Over the dress she wore a tan, quilted car coat. It gets cold in that arena at night.

"The trouble with taking a cab somewhere is that then you have to take another cab back. And by the time you're ready to do that, they're a little hard to come by."

"You really think ahead a lot, don't you?" she asked.

"Sure do. That's part of setting up my life to avoid the knocks."

She swung her free hand around to give me a punch to the stomach. From most girls, a punch to the stomach is nothing to worry about. From Allison—look out. I realized what she was doing just in time—thank God—to stiffen my midsection or she might have dropped me to the grass. When she hit me, we were just in front of the pottery stall where I'd met Jo Sommers the night before. A couple had just moved away from there, and Jo's friend, Nikki, witnessed the blow to my gut with a little look of apprehension. I led Allison over to the stall.

"That's nothing," I told Nikki. "You should see what she can do when she really means it. Allison, this is Nikki. She's a friend of Jo Sommers. This is where I ran into her last night. And Nikki's the one who sold me the coffee mug."

They said hello, and Allison looked at the merchandise while Nikki and I chatted for a moment about Jo Sommers. I told her I'd been to see her and what the status of things seemed to be. Nikki said how awful the murder was, but she didn't sound as if she thought it was really that awful.

I guess I'd been so gaga running into Jo the night before that I hadn't realized what a stark face Nikki had. It wasn't unattractive, exactly. It was long and narrow, but she had a wide-open look about her eyes that made her seem to hover between astonishment and fright. Despite the way Jo had grabbed my attention, I was a little surprised at myself that I hadn't noticed that quality about Nikki the night before.

"What will happen to her?" Nikki asked.

"If she didn't do it, like she says, then hopefully nothing will happen to her, beyond having to spend a couple of nights in jail. She said something about getting an attorney, and I plan to do a little poking around into things myself, after the weekend."

"Who could have killed him?"

She asked this with a little more intensity than I

felt it merited, coming from somebody who was supposed to be mostly worried about the jam a woman friend was in.

"I wouldn't know. But I'm acquainted with the homicide investigator on the case. He's a good man. I expect he'll find out sooner or later. Nice talking to you again."

Allison had been waiting patiently. I took her arm and we started on toward the arena gates.

"Mr. Bragg?"

It was Nikki again. I stopped and turned. She was standing at her stall with one hand raised to her mouth, as if she'd called my name louder than she'd meant to. Her face was screwed up even more than it had been, but then she just shook her head.

"I'm sorry," she said. "It's nothing."

Allison had disengaged her arm and continued on toward the entrance. I hesitated a minute, but then nodded and trailed after Allison. I had a feeling that when I began to look seriously into the murder of Dr. Haywood Somm_ers, Nikki would be one of the persons it would be worth my while to talk to.

With one thing and another, it was almost midnight when we arrived at Gus Wakefield's anniversary party. They lived back in the valley drained by the Carmel River. It's a rural area that provides a way of life for the horsey set. Along with the small clothing store where I buy an occasional pair of jeans, it has a modest shopping center, a golf and country club that looks a little haughty from the road and a tennis ranch that's very popular in that part of the world.

Wakefield lived in a home of stone slab, redwood and glass piled on three levels along the side of a hill overlooking what I guessed would be a view of a fair amount of the Valley, during daylight hours. We could hear music from the house when we still were a hundred yards down the hill. Cars were parked off on both sides of the road. I found an empty space up near the house. It was late enough so that some of the earlier guests had already come and gone.

A tall black youth wearing a tuxedo was acting as doorman, whether to add a touch of class or to keep out the riffraff, I didn't know. The entrance was at one end of the long house. We were directed down a short hallway that had an elevator along the way for easy transportation to the upper levels of the home. The hallway emptied into what might have been the world's largest living room. The rugs were rolled up, a five-piece combo was playing at the far end of the room, and a bar was set up along the wall opposite the windows. There was still a gang of people there, older folks, for the most part. The women wore formal gowns, and the men, most of them, were in military uniforms.

"I'm speechless," Allison murmured in my ear.

"If I'd known it was going to be a theme event, I'd have worn my little sailor suit," I told her.

"You told me you were an enlisted man," said Allison. "These gents are all officers. That's probably the reason for the doorman. In your sailor suit, he wouldn't have let you in."

Gus Wakefield had spotted us and was approaching with a sprightly-looking little woman with a grand smile who turned out to be his wife. There were introductions and small talk before another late-arriving couple came in behind us. The man was in an admiral's dress white uniform and the woman was in gray bangs and black satin. Gus pointed us toward the bar and turned back to the newcomers. Gus himself was in an army uniform with two stars on the shoulders, which made him a major general, if memory served correctly.

There was a lot of vigorous dancing going on out on the floor. Older couples they might be, but their movements were all vigor and youth. It occurred to me that Gus Wakefield might be a very wise man.

The combo had been playing something familiar but vague, and now segued into "Don't Sit Under the Apple Tree," a World War II ditty. Fellows wearing a lot of stars and bars on their collars were doing a measured jitterbug to it. They and the gowned ladies going through the paces with them were grinning.

"This is weird," said Allison.

"I think it's a great idea," I told her.

She looked at me with that look of hers, and I ordered us a couple of drinks. The chap doing the pouring was a handsome youth in his late twenties wearing black trousers and a white steward's jacket. He had curly black hair, a ready smile and an appreciative glance for Allison. He handed across the drinks with a little bow.

"Don't you have a tip glass?" I asked.

"Nice of you to notice, sir. General Wakefield wouldn't allow it. But he did say it would be all right for a bit of discreet palming on the guests' departure."

"That means he really was a general? And these other gentlemen were the rank of the uniforms they're wearing here tonight?"

"Absolutely, sir. These might not be the authentic threads themselves, you understand. A fellow's body does change over the years, I've been told."

Allison snickered.

"But what they wear is what they were," the bartender continued. "What were you? A spy?"

"I wasn't even in the war these people probably were in. I'm Pete, and this is Allison," I told him, extending a hand.

We shook, but his eyes and grin were for Allison. "I'm Alex. Pleased to meet you both. And Allison, if he ever mistreats you, I'd love to be your pal."

Allison smiled. Alex winked, but at me. He was a lad with a charming manner.

"What do you do when you're not hiring out for parties?" I asked. "Or are you family?"

"Not family. And what I do is more of the same, for regular pay and hours in Carmel, at a little place just off Ocean Avenue. It's called the Duck's Quack."

"That's an awful name," I told him.

"I agree," he said, "but they let me keep a tip jar in view there."

We moved away. The combo was taking a break, and several of the guests had gathered around a piano in the corner. A man with a shiny pate wearing a navy captain's whites was banging out a rendition of another tune they used to play and sing in the 1940s that had a refrain advising young warriors to *"Love them all, love them all . . . The long and the short and the tall . . ."* only you could tell from the way the fellows singing around the piano looked at their women that love wasn't the operative word they really used to sing when gathered around the pianos of their past.

We drifted around some, having bits of conversation with various couples, most of whom I didn't catch the names of. When we needed fresh drinks, I let Allison go fetch them so she could flirt with Alex and briefly escape the feeling she was at the retirement-home sock hop.

During one of these forays, I noticed a man I'd been introduced to by Billy Carpenter at the Hunt Club the night before. He and another fellow were talking, and they both of them seemed to be staring in my direction. They turned away when I caught their eyes. The man I'd been introduced to was named Pitt. He was a stocky fellow with a crewcut and was wearing a navy officer's uniform. The larger man he was talking to was in the dress blues of a marine officer. I was tempted to go over and join them to see if it ruffled them, but I was distracted right then by a portly man in the uniform of an army colonel who took a pratfall over in front of the bar. He'd tripped while carrying a tray of glasses filled with champagne, and the floor around him now was all sticky and fizzy and filled with pieces of glass.

Alex was around the bar in a jiffy, helping the merrily chuckling colonel to his feet. Somebody else was mopping up the mess. Allison had been crossing the room toward me with fresh drinks when it happened. She had stopped and turned to stare, but now continued over to me.

"Didn't I see something like this years ago in *La Dolce Vita?*" she asked.

I took the drink with a shrug. "You have to remember, there was a time when these aging gentlemen were the toast of the land. Trim, handsomely decked out, much sought after socially, when they were home. Those memories are hard to put down into the cold ground, until the body itself goes."

Gus Wakefield and his wife approached us again. Mrs. Wakefield began a conversation with Allison while the general turned me slightly to one side and tried to pump me about what Jo Sommers had to tell me at the county jail when I visited her. I gave him a bare-bones account of what both Jo and detective Wally Hamlin had told me. I didn't mention anything about the tape-recorded domestic quarrel.

"I hear the local district attorney, Thackery, is a bit of a hardhead," I told him.

He took a breath but didn't reply right away. He looked off in the distance. "I don't know the man, personally," he told me. "I have heard he's ambitious. Why?"

"I have it on good authority he'd like to hang the doctor's murder on Jo. Tidy it up and get it over with in a hurry. Why do you suppose he'd want to do that?"

Wakefield looked back at me sharply. "Assuming that Mrs. Sommers is innocent, you mean."

I nodded. "Until last night, it had been years since I'd seen Mrs. Sommers, but I still consider her a friend. She told me today she didn't do it. I have to believe her until I find something a lot more convincing than Thackery has found so far."

"Well, I suppose..." began Wakefield, his voice trailing off as he stared into his glass. "I was only going to say..."

But he hesitated again, and before he could resume, we were joined by another one of the men I'd met the night before. Tonight he was wearing navy whites. He was the short, compact man named Whitey.

"I believe you two met last evening," said Wakefield, with a hearty boom, as if he'd just been saved from having to tell me something nasty. "Commander Whiteman, Peter Bragg."

We shook hands again.

"Mr. Bragg here has been doing some preliminary investigation of the Sommers murder," Wakefield told him.

The commander's gray eyebrows arched quickly. "Indeed? And what seems to have gone on out there last night? Awful thing to have happen."

I nodded. "The doctor apparently suffocated. Somebody held a pillow over his face while he was slowed down by drink."

"I heard they were holding Mrs. Sommers," said the commander. "Absolutely incredible, if I'm any judge of character. Couldn't the man just have got-

ten so swizzled he choked all by himself? He drank
enough, I've heard."

"The police seem to think somebody else was
involved. But I'm glad you feel the way you do
about Mrs. Sommers. I think she's innocent, myself."

"Of course she is," he said, staring off. "Ah!
Excuse me. Have to see Pitt about a golf game." He
moved off with a brisk stride, over to the two men I'd
noticed staring at me earlier.

"Excuse me, General . . ."

Wakefield waved a hand in dismissal. "Forget the
uniform. Call me Gus."

"Okay, Gus. Do you know the two men Whitey's
talking to now? I believe the man in Navy whites was
at the Hunt Club last night with you and Billy
Carpenter."

"That's right, Lawrence Pitt. He and Whitey were
both DD skippers, in the war."

"Destroyers?"

"Yep. You know, it's a funny thing. I never thought
of it before, until seeing the two of them together in
their uniforms like that. They're both of short stature.
Maybe it took that sort of man, with the little-man
pugnacity, a bit of the bulldog, to handle those ships
properly. Did a job for the army, I'll tell you. One of
them saved Omaha Beach for us."

"I didn't know that."

"Oh, yes. Steamed right in toward shore to knock
out some gun positions nobody else could get at. It
was a very touch-and-go situation there until the
navy saved the day."

"I see. How about the other man, in the marine
uniform."

"That's George Whittle. Korea was his war. Then
he was in advertising, up in San Francisco, before he
retired and moved down here. Larry Pitt stayed in
the navy for thirty years. Dabbled in real estate down

here some after that. Whitey did more than dabble. Began acquiring property all over the place. Wheeled and dealed. He made a good deal of money. Mostly retired now, like the rest of us. Has a house in Pacific Grove, a cabin down the coast and a place in Palm Springs, that I know of."

"How nice for him."

"I know what you mean," Wakefield chuckled. "I'm comfortable enough, myself, but Commander Smith is really well at ease."

"Gus, if you wouldn't mind, I'd like to get back for a moment to what you were going to tell me about the district attorney. I had asked you why you felt he might want to try to convict Mrs. Sommers for her husband's murder."

"Well, actually no, that really wasn't what I was about to say. Maybe Mrs. Sommers is the only sort of suspect he has. But I had been thinking of something further along, that had been triggered by your question. I had asked myself why anybody at all would want to kill Dr. Sommers."

"And what was your conclusion?"

He leveled a forceful gaze at me. "I don't know that I should even verbalize such random thoughts."

"I wish you would. I promised my lady friend here I wouldn't start looking into this thing seriously until after the weekend. But now is a timely opportunity. You know this community. I'm an interloper. I'll need help."

He lowered his gaze again to the glass in his hand. "Well, it's something you're apt to think of yourself sometime anyway, I suppose. But understand, this is little more than speculation. Dr. Sommers was a psychiatrist who specialized in the problems encountered by the military. As you might appreciate, there can be terrible anguish generated in men who go to war."

"I know, sir."

"All right. It's just, then, some of the men Dr. Sommers helped, or tried to help over the years, quite probably live in the Monterey area now. Dr. Sommers could perhaps know about the bleaker sides to any number of us. He could cause a great deal of mischief in the community if he were of a mind to." Wakefield shrugged. "Or, maybe he just triggered memories in somebody who could not tolerate having those memories stirred up. That's all I was thinking. Probably not worth the breath to mention it, even."

Chapter 6 ─────────

Thanks to Gus Wakefield's party, Allison and I were running even later on Sunday than we had been on Saturday night. We had to put off some of the sightseeing I had wanted to do in order to get to the Sunday afternoon concert at the fairgrounds. We were nearly an hour late as it was.

The Sunday afternoon concerts are especially important, both to me and the Monterey Jazz Festival. They are the future of this kind of music. The performers are teenaged kids from high schools throughout Northern California. For the past dozen years or so, the festival has sponsored a high school competition in the spring. The school bands and combos are judged by professional jazz musicians, and the winning groups are invited to take part at the jazz festival in the fall. In addition, all of the youngsters are invited to audition for a chair in the year's California High School All-Star Jazz Ensemble. Those who make the cut, about nineteen kids in all, spend an intensive six days prior to the festival in rehearsals, working with jazz professionals like Bill Berry, Bob Brookmeyer and Freddie Hubbard.

These, then, are the youngsters who provide the music Sunday afternoons. And they are very good. And as at the concert the afternoon before, people get up and dance in the broad, earthen aisles, while the rest of us stretch out in the sun drinking beer and listening to the music and the occasional full-throated roar of a twin-engine jet airliner taking off from Monterey County Airport, just down the road.

When we stepped into the Hunt Club after the performance, we had a surprise waiting for us. Jo Sommers was sitting by herself at a corner table, wearing the blue pants suit she'd had on Friday night when they'd taken her into custody. When she saw us, she got up and made her way through the smoke and din of the crowded room.

"Welcome back to the world," I told her.

She managed a weak smile and gave Allison the once-over. I did the introductions.

"Did Thackery decide he didn't have a case?" I asked her.

"Not at all. That man is a monster. But I have a sharp little feminist lawyer who makes him feel uncomfortable. No charges have been filed yet, but he said I could expect that to happen by the end of next week. They released me just a bit ago. I came by here hoping to find you."

Jo turned to Allison. "Peter gave me your message yesterday, and I appreciated it. Really. And I know the weekend isn't over yet, but there's a few hours until the next concert, and I wondered if you could come by my home for just a little while. Both of you."

She turned her attention back to me now. "I want to tell you about a thing or two, but not here. And after talking to my lawyer, I think I need your help more than ever."

I glanced at Allison. She made a slight movement with one shoulder that I took as acquiescence. We left the Hunt Club. Jo had come to the fairgrounds in a cab, so she rode the rest of the way home with Allison and me. We all of us tried to make small talk on the drive over the hill and south to Carmel

Highlands, but it was a strain, and we realized it eventually and contented ourselves with staring out the windows.

Once home, Jo said hello to the noisy cat, then excused herself and went into the bathroom to freshen up. Allison and I went into the front room and looked out the large front windows at the Pacific Ocean and talked in whispers as if we were in church.

"She is, as you said," murmured Allison, "an, ahem, attractive woman."

"Noticed that, did you?"

"And she has, as they say where I come from, eyes for you."

"I suspect she has eyes for any man who can still get around without dragging one leg."

"No, Bragg. Nice try, but you're special to her."

"Sure, I'm special, because of my line of work. She's in a jam and wants me to help her out of it."

"What do you think she wants to tell you?"

"Tell us. I'm not working yet. Anything she has to say she can say in the presence of both of us."

She was standing alongside me staring out the window, but she raised a hand and gave my arm a little squeeze. "What do you think she wants to tell us?"

"Probably something her feminist lawyer put into her head. But it'll have to be brief, whatever it is. This joint makes me jumpy."

"Me too."

Jo Sommers came back into the room then, and she didn't act as if she intended to be brief. She took one of those foot-long wooden fireplace matches out of a cardboard canister on the mantel and lit the pile of paper and logs in the big fireplace. Then she crossed to a cabinet in the corner that opened into a wet bar and brought out a bucket of ice from a refrigerated compartment.

"Let me fix you a drink," she said. "I intend to have a walloping big Scotch, myself, but we have most everything."

Allison and I exchanged glances. "Maybe just one, Jo, but we've got other things to do. We really can't stay for very long."

"I know. I'll be as brief as I can."

Allison and I each had a gin and tonic. We settled a little ways apart on a sofa at one end of the room. Jo Sommers poured out about a cup of Scotch over some ice in a big balloon glass and settled in a nearby easy chair, tucking her long, slender legs beneath her and lighting a cigarette. Then she got right into it.

"Background, first," she told us. "I don't remember how much I told you the other night, Peter. We didn't seem to have talked for very long." A brief glance at Allison with that. "But Woody, my husband, spent nearly twenty years in the army, treating men who'd been in battle, and others who encountered problems of one sort or another in peacetime. Not that he was seeing patients eight hours a day or anything like that. He did a great deal of teaching, as well, and originated various programs. And he was good enough at what he did so his duties weren't just restricted to army personnel. He worked with the navy and air force as well. He put in a stint at the Pentagon in Washington. When he left the military, he spent another dozen or so years in private practice, but his work wasn't all that different. Much of it was on contract with the Veterans Administration and other government bodies. Other patients sought him out because of his reputation. He had a good practice and made money at it."

She quieted a moment, drawing on the Newport, swirling the Scotch in the glass and staring at the carpet between us. "The problem is," she continued quietly, "I'm not going to see very much of that."

She raised her eyes with a little smile. "I met Woody late on. He was married and divorced once before. His former wife died last year, but he has a son and a daughter. They get the bulk of the estate. Also what government insurance he had. He took out another insurance policy, a term policy naming me as beneficiary. It's for one hundred thousand dollars. He said it should be enough to put any girl back on her feet. But my lady lawyer told me it's going to be a battle royal to collect from the insurance company so long as I'm suspected of murdering my husband."

She moved one leg out from beneath her and let it swing idly along the front of her chair. She put out the Newport, lowered her eyes and swirled her Scotch some more. Then she had a long drink of it.

"I have no resources of my own," she said. "Aside from my wardrobe and a few houshold possessions and some bits of jewelry that Woody bought me."

"What about the house?" I asked.

"It's in both our names, but it has a whopping mortgage on it. I'll have to put it on the market, even if I get the insurance money. Just not so quickly, is all."

"Didn't he have any sort of mortgage insurance that would pay it off if he died?"

Jo looked up at me with a bitter little smile. It had enough venom in it to bring a squirmy movement from Allison.

"No. No mortgage insurance, dirt cheap as it is. Woody did that deliberately."

And with that, she got serious about drinking the Scotch. She'd had one or two good tugs at it, but now she drained the glass.

"Excuse me," she said quietly, getting to her feet.

She crossed the room to the bar again, and while she had her back to us I glanced at Allison, and Allison shot me a child's face of horror, mouth agape and eyes bugging. She did it in about a tenth of a second, then once again assumed that placid look of vague dreaminess and mild interest she showed the world at large on most occasions.

I smiled and waited while Jo Sommers tossed in another couple of cubes of ice and transferred the rest of the Scotch from the bottle into the large glass. She came back to her chair, but this time put down the glass onto a small table beside her and crossed over to poke at a couple of blazing logs in the fireplace. Then she sat back down and leaned forward.

"You see," she continued, "Woody had his own view of the world and the people in it. I don't suppose a man, or anybody else for that matter, can spend thirty years of his life dealing with people who have deep neuroses and other illnesses I haven't even heard of, without taking on what one might call a few peculiar traits of their own. Woody felt my place was in the home, so long as he was here to share it. But if something were to happen to him, he felt my place should be out of the home, at least this home. And since he was, as kindly as I can put it, a few years older than myself, it could be expected that he might pass into the great beyond some time before I did. Not that either of us expected it quite this soon, nor, lord knows, in such dramatic fashion. But whenever it happened, he didn't feel I should retain such an imposing home to call my own."

"Why on earth not?" asked Allison.

Another little smile from Jo. "He felt it would over-enhance my status."

Allison looked at her with astonishment.

"His very words," Jo continued. "He felt it was all

right for me to be a part of the place, like one of the back rooms or the ice plant out front, so long as he was lord and master and obviously provider of the walls. He felt it was too much grandness to be in the possession of a single woman who hadn't made much of a mark in life before meeting and hooking up with the renowned Dr. Sommers. The pig."

Allison and I exchanged uneasy glances while Jo tilted the glass to her mouth.

"Where is all this taking us?" I asked.

She nodded her head, acknowledging it was a fair question. "I would like anything you can do for me to be on a little more businesslike basis than either of us might have originally meant it to be. Instead of an acquaintance from the past spending a few hours of his time doing the poor girl a favor, I would like for you to go into this the same as you would for any of your clients."

"I would have done that anyway."

"I mean, I want to hire you, Peter. Specifically to find out who killed Woody. It won't be enough for the district attorney to decide he doesn't have a good enough case against me to get a conviction. I have to prove to the insurance company that somebody else did it. Otherwise I might have to sue the insurance company. And you know how much that sort of thing could eat into the one hundred thousand dollars."

"Considerably," I agreed.

"Jo, don't you have any family who can help you?" Allison asked.

Jo took out another Newport, tamped one end on the table beside her, then lit it and blew away a small cloud of smoke. "I have a brother, and my mother, up in the state of Washington. He's a dairy farmer. Yes, I've been in touch with them, and they're willing to loan me whatever it takes to hire myself a competent private detective to get me out of the mess I'm in. You are competent, aren't you, Peter?"

"He's a very competent private detective," Allison said quietly. "He's so competent it almost destroyed our relationship before it had a chance to get off the ground."

"You'll have to tell me about that sometime," Jo said, looking away so you couldn't tell whom she was talking to.

"One thing you should keep in mind, though, Jo," I told her. "Regular law enforcement agencies usually have more expertise and manpower, and are in a far better position to find a killer than just a single, free-lance detective."

"Maybe so. But my attorney told me the police have different priorities than does somebody who's suspected of murdering her husband. I want somebody I know is on my side and working full time at it."

"What I mean, though, is that you shouldn't hold back anything from the police just because you hire me."

"I've already told the police everything I've told you, and that's all there is to tell."

She'd only had a couple of drags off the cigarette, but now she put it out in the ashtray, as if making a little period to her statement. She swirled the Scotch, made a little toss of her head to flounce back her hair, and raised the glass to her lips.

I glanced at Allison. The heels of her sandals were making a silent little drumbeat on the Chinese rug, and she gave me a hopeful look. She was ready to get out of there.

"Jo, just two questions, then we have to get moving along."

"All right."

"Had you noticed anything at all different in your

husband's activities lately? Unusual phone calls, things in the mail, the hours he came and went..."

Jo made a little wave of her hand. "No. My husband's life was bone-achingly predictable. He spent most of his time right here, when he wasn't playing golf or attending some social function. That county detective, Wally somebody, asked me the same thing."

"Okay, then my last question. What was the temper of things between your husband and yourself?"

That brought her up short. "Hey, wait a minute. If I'm the one paying you, you're on my side, right?"

"Of course. But a change in one portion of a person's life can sometimes mask a change in another part. All I'm doing is asking my first question from a different direction."

"Oh. Well, no. Things between us were about the same as they've been for a good long while."

I let it sit there a moment to see if she'd take it any further. She didn't. Allison was beginning to twitch.

"Okay," I said, getting to my feet. I had a head start, but Allison was on her feet with a contented smile before I was standing straight.

"As long as you're out of the bucket," I told Jo, "there isn't the same minute-to-minute urgency to all this that there was before, so tomorrow I'd like to combine a little pleasure with business. I won't charge you for the day, but I'll be thinking about things, and maybe do some initial poking around. But I'd also like to do a little sightseeing with Allison before having to put her on a bus or plane and send her home alone. We've already lost some time together because of your husband's death."

"Kindly put," said Jo. She rose and walked us to the front door. "Sure, have some fun tomorrow. I'm sorry I've taken away from your weekend."

"Hey, no problem," said Allison. "I hope things

work out for you. I'm sure Petey will give it the old college try."

"I certainly hope so," Jo told her, opening the door and extending a hand toward Allison. "It was nice meeting you. Maybe we can get together some-time and do girl things together when this is all over with."

"Sure, I'd like that," said Allison, taking Jo's hand in both of her own. "Good luck."

She scampered down the stairs and crossed to my car.

"And you," Jo said. "I suppose I'll be seeing you around the old farm, sometime."

"Of course. Look, it might be a good idea for you to lie low for a day or so, until I can get some kind of direction on this thing."

"Lie low?"

"Stay around home here as much as you can, more as a watchdog than anything else. Make a note of any strangers you might see, anything else of a suspicious nature."

"You think I might be in some sort of danger?"

"Not likely. But if anything does happen to fright-en or disturb you, call Wally Hamlin and tell him about it. If anything special comes up you think I should know about, leave word at my motel." I took out a card I'd picked up in the motel office and wrote my room number on the back.

"Can I have friends in, if I start getting cabin fever?"

"Women friends, sure. The other sort might be a little indiscreet."

She took the card and just stood there staring at me for a moment. "All right, I'll do what you say, Daddy." And with that she gave me a wink and a little kiss through the air, then closed the door.

Down in the car, Allison was sitting in the passenger seat with her eyes closed. She had the radio on, playing some sort of twangy country song at high volume. I turned it down and started the engine.

"Petey?" I growled, pulling away from the curb. "You've never called me Petey before in your life."

Allison gave me the little ladylike snort she resorts to from time to time. "Women sometimes behave in front of other women," she told me, "in a fashion in which they would not behave if not in front of other women. Hey, listen, Bragg, I was in enemy territory in there. I could feel it in my bones."

"Jealousy stuff?"

"Oh, sure, a little of that. You have to expect it among two reasonably attractive women and a reasonably attractive male. But this isn't all me-and-you, and her-and-you, and her-and-me stuff. There's something apart from all that. Something that just doesn't ring true."

"I'd be a pretty bum detective if I hadn't noticed it myself."

Chapter 7 —————

The bit of sightseeing Allison and I had planned to do that afternoon was out of the question by now. We went back to the motel to clean up and have some of the gin in the refrigerator and pretend we were just a carefree couple down for a fun weekend, but memories of Jo Sommers and her dead husband kept intruding. We would be carrying on a reasonably normal conversation, then one of us would trail off and stare into the distance.

If a person is serious about taking in the jazz festival, there isn't much time for elegant dining. We decided to have a couple of cheeseburgers at a snug and friendly little bar and restaurant in Carmel named after writer Jack London, but before eating, we searched out the Duck's Quack, to see if Alex, the personable bartender from Gus Wakefield's party, was on duty. He was on duty, but we didn't stick around to have a drink. The place was crowded. The bar was packed, and out on the floor, we would have had to share a table with other people. Neither of us felt like doing that right then. One other thing we noted, which seemed a bit odd, was that when he wasn't mixing drinks for the bar customers or a pair of cocktail waitresses, Alex was in what looked like a serious discussion with Nikki, Jo Sommers's girl friend who ran the pottery stall at the fairgrounds. The reason it seemed odd was that the shopkeepers outside the arena don't shut down their stalls between concerts. There are two other areas on the grounds where small jazz groups provide free concerts throughout the day and into the evening, and there are always enough people around to provide a brisk business at the food stands and merchandise stalls.

When we got back out to the fairgrounds, we saw that Nikki had already packed up her goods and abandoned the stall. She was the only shopkeeper there to have done so.

Two hours later we were in our chairs on the arena floor, applauding the set just concluded by that year's assembly of Monterey Jazz Festival All-Stars that included Shelly Manne on drums and Clark Terry on trumpet. My companion turned to me with a sober expression and said, "It just came to me. I think that woman Jo is in the business of stealing people's souls."

It was about as whacky a comment I'd ever heard from Allison, but in a curious way I thought I knew what she meant. My thoughts about Jo Sommers had never been that far-ranging when she used to come into the No Name. They never got much beyond the stage of trying to imagine what joy it would be to get into bed with her. But it occurred to me now that there was a dark side to her nature which Allison had just commented on. It could be the dangerous side of a person's character that would always attract some well-meaning dummy like myself, who thought he only lusted after her body. I was thinking all this when I realized Allison and I had been staring at each other for some moments.

"I think you might be right, and maybe I should kick the job," I told her.

"You can't do that. You'd regret it for the rest of

your life. But I don't think I can listen to any more
music tonight. Let's go get pie-eyed somewhere."

And that's how we managed to get our minds off
of Jo Sommers for the rest of the evening.

Monday morning, after staring out the motel window
for another twenty minutes, Allison got her sketch. I
had just finished shaving and stepped out of the
bathroom. She was poised with her pad on her knees;
she cocked her head, and made about three dozen lines
with some kind of pencil she uses. It took less than a
minute, but she finally turned to me with a big grin.

"Got it!"

I looked over her shoulder, and she did indeed
have it, though my eye isn't good enough to tell
what she'd put in and what she'd left out, but the
drawing captured not only the appearance but the
fresh air, sea tang and cypress-smell mood of the
view from that upper-room window at the white inn
with green shutters in Carmel.

"Great hands," I told her.

"Huh? Oh, yeah. Thanks."

It put her in a fine mood for the rest of the day.
We took a walk down along the beach road, then
wended up through a pleasant residential area in the
shallow hills above. I purposely led her around to a
two-story, Spanish mission-style home with white stucco walls and red tile roof not far from the motel we
were staying at. By Carmel standards there was nothing outstanding about the place except for a plaque
set in a large block of white stone to one side of the
narrow driveway. I pointed it out and Allison bent
over to read the inscription:

> *Stilwell House*
> *Home of Joseph Warren Stilwell*
> *"Vinegar Joe"*

General, U.S.Army   1883–1946
A soldier without peer who never deviated in his absolute
dedication to The United States of America

She looked up at me.

"Ever heard of him?" I asked.

"Vaguely. Who was he?"

"Pretty much what the plaque says. He was a very good soldier who was put into an impossible situation that called more for a politician. He was American adviser to Generalissimo Chiang Kai-shek in China during World War Two. Stilwell thought all the money and supplies this country pumped into China in those days should have been used to equip and train a first-rate army that then would go out and kill Japanese troops who were occupying a large portion of that country."

"Sounds logical."

"Unfortunately, the generalissimo had other ideas. It was a frustrating war for Stilwell. Barbara Tuchman wrote a book about him. I have it at home. There's a photo of him right here in the side yard with a bunch of reporters. It was his swan song press conference. This is the home he retired to. Not much more than a year later he was dead."

Allison moved off a little ways, staring at the stucco walls. "You have a feeling for the place."

"I have great feeling for the memory of the general. Whenever I'm down in this area, I like to come by and look at the home that was his. It's a little bit like going to church was when I was a kid."

"I'll sketch it for you sometime, if you'd like."

"I'd like."

We had breakfast up in town and decided to drive down the coast to Big Sur country. We were on our way back to the car when I thought about the office. I hadn't told anybody I wouldn't be showing up that

morning, so I ducked into a patio ringed with shops
and used a pay phone there to call Ceejay, the office
secretary and traffic director.

"You must be having a nice time," Ceejay said
when I told her I wasn't sure when I'd be back.

"We're having a grand time," I told her. "We're
going to spend another day sightseeing. After that,
I'll be working. Somebody I know from the past is in
some trouble. I told her I'd try to help her out."

"Her name isn't Nikki, is it?"

"Nikki? No. What made you think so?"

"Somebody by that name phoned the office before
anybody was in this morning. The answering service
took the call. She left a number. It's in the four-oh-
eight area. That's where you're at, isn't it?"

"Yes, and maybe I know the girl. I met one named
Nikki who's a friend of the girl who's in trouble. Did
she leave a message?"

"She wants you to call her. Said it was urgent. The
girl at the answering service said she sounded
distraught. Nikki told her that she didn't want to
sound corny, but that you should be told it really
could be a matter of life or death. End of message."

"Better give me the number. I'll see if I can reach
her."

When I tried dialing the number that had been
left with the answering service, nobody picked up
the phone. I called the Sommers residence. Jo
answered on the second ring. I asked if she'd spoken
to Nikki that morning.

"No, I haven't spoken to anybody. Why?"

"She might have been trying to reach me. It doesn't
matter. How have things been around there?"

"Not nice. I had a heavy case of insomnia, followed
by some of the worst nightmares I've ever had. I
think I'll spend most of the day in the hot tub. You
could come by and join me."

She was doing it again, but it was harmless enough over the telephone. At least I thought it was.

"With Allison, of course," I told her.

"Of course. Provided she's willing to take off her clothes and soak naked with the rest of us."

"You don't wear a swimsuit?"

"Of course not, Peter. That's not the California way."

I finally got off the phone. Allison, slightly nettled, was looking into nearby shop windows.

"What took so long?" she asked.

"I checked in with the office. They'd had a call from somebody down here named Nikki. It might be the girl from the pottery stall. She sounded as if she might be in a jam of some kind. I tried calling her but didn't get an answer, so I checked with Jo Sommers, but she hadn't talked with Nikki today."

Allison gave sort of a grunt, and after that she didn't have much to say as we made our way down south to Big Sur. It might or might not have been a moody reaction to my call to Jo Sommers.

The drive south of Carmel is pretty breathtaking, one of the most spectacular stretches along the entire California coastline. The shoulder rubbing between a couple of tectonic plates along the San Andreas Fault that made most of the state a potential earthquake disaster area also created the upwelling of earth that formed the coastal range of hills. The highway that traversed them along this part of the coast ran from several hundred feet above the Pacific to nearly sea level, rising and plunging down long canyons inland, soaring across gorges on deeply vaulted bridges, crossing great slabs of grassland that sheer off to the sea.

It is almost too spectacular. The first time I drove down that road I nearly plunged off it in a couple of places. I pay more attention to my driving now, but if you're in the passenger seat, it's some treat. Cattle ranches are scattered here and there along the way, but once you get to the Big Sur country, about twenty-five miles south of Carmel, most of the countryside is state or federal wilderness protection areas.

After a couple of side excursions, I drove to Nepenthe, a restaurant and bar in a building that used to be the private residence of Orsen Welles and Rita Hayworth. At least that's what they tell you. It's built into the side of a gorge about a quarter of a mile back from the shoreline and several hundred feet above sea level. But that's still not very high compared with the surroundings. Inland, across coast Highway 1, brown, hummocky hills, scarred with trenches formed by heavy winter rains and speckled with grass and scrub brush, climb several hundred feet higher. Nepenthe has a couple of patios on different levels, both of them looking out over the sea and hills and sky, with the watchful turkey buzzards circling overhead.

And like most facilities open to the public in remote stretches of California, Nepenthe has a gift shop, in a separate building down on the parking lot level. It sells everything from jewelry and brass to sheepskin clothing and books. Allison, like most women I've known, felt compelled to devote a half hour or more going through the shop. I stuck it out for about ten minutes then climbed the stairs and took a steep upward path to the main building that houses the restaurant and bar. I was sipping a Bloody Mary on the main patio when Allison showed up, and we went inside for lunch. And after we ate, I finally reached Nikki on the telephone.

"Thank God, Mr. Bragg. Thank you for calling."

The girl at the answering service had been right. Nikki was upset.

"I've got to see you," she told me. "There's something terribly wrong. I think somebody wants to kill me."

"What makes you think that?"

"I—it would sound silly if I tried to tell you over the phone. Jo told me you're a private detective. I don't have a whole lot of money, but I thought... Well, maybe you could just advise me. I've never been in anything like this in my life."

"It sounds like something you maybe should go to the police about."

"No, I can't do that."

"Does this have anything to do with Jo? Or her husband's murder, do you think?"

"It might. I can drive up to Carmel or Monterey or wherever you are. Right now, if it would be convenient."

"I'm not at Carmel. I'm at Nepenthe."

"Even better. I live down here. Do you know where Fernwood is?"

"You mean that cluster of buildings just before you get to Pfeiffer State Park?"

"That's it. I live back in a canyon near there. Could we meet at the restaurant there?"

"Sure, but I'm with a friend, and I wanted to show her another place or two before we headed back north. How about three o'clock?"

"That'll be fine."

"Okay, see you then."

"Mr. Bragg?"

"Yes?"

"I don't want to sound like such a ninny, but I'm really frightened. If I'm not there, at the restaurant, by a few minutes after three, maybe you could come check up on things here where I live... My last name is Scarborough. The people at the restaurant know me and can give you directions. 'Bye."

She didn't even wait for me to reply before hanging up.

Allison had been back in the restroom. She caught the last of the conversation on her way out.

"You reached her?"

"Yes. She's a very frightened girl. Said somebody might want to kill her. I told her we'd meet her at a place back up the road, later this afternoon."

"Don't you think you should go now?"

"No, she should be safe enough where she is. She lives up a canyon somewhere down here. It's pretty hard to root out places like that if you're not familiar with the area. And there's another place I want to show you while we're down here."

The other place was back up Highway 1 a ways. It was a scattering of lodges up in a fold of the high coastal hills. It was said to be a favorite getaway spot for a lot of the Hollywood theatrical crowd and various other eccentrics out of Southern California. I'd stopped in their restaurant one night around ten o'clock for an after-dinner drink and thought I'd stumbled onto a Halloween party. It turned out to be the fashionable hour for the lodge guests to eat. They were in their twenties and thirties, for the most part, all platform shoes, bright, flaring clothes, heavy cosmetics and exaggerated hair styles.

The place is more sedate during the day. Their restaurant also has an outside patio where you can stare at the hills and sky. Allison wasn't all that impressed. You can only absorb so much of that kind of scenery without becoming jaded or feeling like you want to hurl yourself off the nearest cliff. So as it turned out, Allison had been right, back at Nepenthe. We should have gone looking for Nikki Scarborough sooner.

Chapter 8 —————————

Fernwood was one of those wide places in the road with a gas station and small grocery store, a couple of motels, a nearby campground and the restaurant where I told Nikki I'd meet her. We got there about five minutes after three. There were a dozen customers in the dining room and an open area out back, and a couple of more people in the bar. Nikki wasn't one of them. A tall woman in her early thirties with a long face and wide mouth that smiled easily was at the cash register giving change to an elderly couple. When the couple left, I asked the woman if she'd seen Nikki Scarborough that afternoon.

"She was just here, but left kind of suddenly," she told me.

"How do you mean?"

"She was sitting at the counter drinking a cup of coffee. I was waiting tables outside. When I came back in she'd left. There was a quarter on the counter next to her half-finished coffee. I looked outside and saw her little red VW leaving like she was late for something. Of course, she always drove like that."

"How long had she been here?"

"About ten minutes."

"And how long ago would you guess that she left?"

"Couldn't have been more than five minutes ago."

"Do you know if she said anything to anybody before she left?"

"I don't know. I'll ask. Hey, is your name Bragg, by the way?"

"Yes, it is."

"Do you have something that proves it?"

I took out my wallet and handed her my driver's license.

"Peter Bragg. You're the one, I guess." She turned to take a manila envelope off the back counter. "She asked me to give this to you if she missed you."

"When she was here just now?"

"That's right."

"We were supposed to meet here. I wonder why she didn't wait to give it to me herself."

"I don't know. She seemed jumpy. But then, Nikki's always been on the nervous side. She's the only person I know who still chews her fingernails. Wait here. I'll see if she said anything to anybody before she left."

Allison looked at me and then at the envelope. "Going to wait until Christmas?"

The flap was sealed. I tore it open and took out a couple of audio tape cassettes. They were marked with a series of letters and numerals that didn't mean anything to me.

"I don't suppose you brought down a tape recorder with you?" I asked Allison.

"I don't even own one. What do you think it's all about?"

"I don't know. But I don't like Nikki leaving here the way she did."

The waitress came back with a shake of her head. "She didn't say boo to anybody. Nobody even noticed when she got up and left. That's not like her. She's a friendly girl. Always says hello and good-bye to us."

I went over to a pay phone and tried dialing Nikki's number. I let it ring for a long time, but nobody answered. I waited until the waitress was free again and told her what Nikki had said about somebody being able to give me directions to where she lived.

"I could, but I don't know if I should. I'm beginning to think something funny's going on."

I took out my wallet and this time showed her the photostat of my investigator's license. "I think you're right," I told her. "Nikki and I met at the jazz festival through a mutual friend. This morning she phoned my office in San Francisco to leave a message for me. I talked to her later by phone and she indicated she had a problem I might be able to help her with. We were supposed to meet here. But she said if she didn't show up, I should get directions to her place and drive on out there."

The girl was nodding her acceptance before I'd finished talking. "Gotcha," she told me. She took a paper napkin out of a dispenser and drew me a crude but adequate map showing how to find the cabin Nikki rented.

While Allison was getting into the car, I unlocked the trunk and took out a small case that carried a .38-caliber revolver inside a clip-on belt holster. There was another case in there with my .45 automatic, but I left that in the trunk. I climbed into the car, took the gun and holster out of the case and transferred it to the glove compartment.

"You think you're going to need that thing?" Allison asked.

"Probably not, but it's like the Amex card commercials."

"You never leave home without it."

"You got it. Maybe just for the hell of it you should hang around here while I drive out to Nikki's. You can flirt with the bartender, or something."

"And become the second person that girl in there knows who still chews her fingernails? Drive, Bragg."

I drove, back down out of the redwood groves and across the easy rolling pastureland to the north.

We came to a small state park and beach on the shoreward side of the highway. Opposite the park was a narrow secondary road that ran on back into the hills to the east. According to the map, we turned up the road and followed it back for about a mile. The waitress had said we'd see Nikki's place off to the left, a weather-faded structure nestled at the base of a steep, low hill covered with brush and wild grass. There would be another nearby structure that Nikki used to manufacture her pottery.

The secondary road wasn't kept in A-1 condition, and I traveled a little faster along it than its designers had anticipated. We did some jouncing around. Allison didn't say anything more but just sat tight-lipped beside me. I hoped we wouldn't find anything amiss at the cabin. Allison has some toughness to her, but not when it comes to violence, in any of its forms. It puts a hammerlock on her psyche and screws up her painting. She had told me that more than once. She said she really shouldn't be going out with a hooligan who ran into the situations I sometimes did. It was one of those things we'd never found a satisfactory way to resolve.

We saw the cabin and outbuilding when we still were a quarter mile down the road. Twin tire tracks led from the road over to the cabin, and at the end of the tracks was a red VW with its driver's side door standing open. I did not like the looks of that. As I braked and turned off the road, I saw the door to the small cabin was standing wide open as well, but I didn't see any sign of Nikki. Allison saw these things as well.

"Pete, I'm worried."

"Me too." I stopped a little ways off from the red

VW, staring around at things, then I put the car back into gear and made a tight circle so my own auto was pointed back toward the road. I braked but left the key in the ignition and the motor running. I took the .38 out of the glove compartment and got out, scanning the area all around us.

"Come around and get in the driver's seat," I told Allison. "If you see anybody at all besides that girl, honk the horn twice and get the hell out of here."

She got out of the car like a shot and came around to the driver's side. She started to get in but then stood up. "I can't do that, just sit there like that."

"Then stand right here and leave the door open. Do not leave here."

"Okay, boss. Call me if you find anything."

I grunted and crossed quickly to the VW. I skirted it all the way around in a circle, my eyes alternating from the ground around the car to the cabin and outbuilding. There didn't seem to be anything around the car I might disturb, so I went over to the open door and looked inside. The car was empty.

I approached the cabin in the same way, cautiously, revolver in hand, eyes trying to take in everything at once. I peered through the open front door. It was sparsely furnished. Nothing seemed in disarray. I called Nikki's name. Nobody answered. I went on inside. The place was mostly one large room, with a bed along the wall to the left and a small kitchen area in back with a stove and refrigerator. Off that was a small bathroom. I went through the place quickly. There wasn't anybody at home, but on the kitchen floor behind the small counter I found a telephone with the receiver off the cradle. The phone was attached to a wall connection, but it wasn't making the whine phones make when you leave the receiver off the hook.

I went back outside and tried to follow the telephone line with my eyes, but it went through some trees out near the road and I couldn't follow it all the way to the utility pole.

Allison stood in a little crouch, her hands on her knees, the way football and baseball coaches are apt to crouch during a tight game. I raised a cautionary hand to keep her back and started to circle the cabin. The door to the outbuilding was secured by a hasp with a padlock on it. I went around behind the cabin, scanning the surrounding hills.

That's when I saw her. Or what I took to be Nikki Scarborough. She was lying facedown about twenty yards up the steep, grassy slope behind the cabin. I went up to her quickly, but I didn't touch the body. There was no need to. She had what looked like a small-caliber entrance wound at the base of her skull. Blood still flowed feebly from the wound, and a small puddle was soaking into the ground next to her turned face. Her right leg was cocked up and her fingers were dug into the ground on either side of her, as if she were trying to claw herself out of harm's way.

"Bragg!" Allison called.

I slid to the ground at a front corner of the cabin and brought up my .38 in a two-handed grip. But Allison was all right and alone. She was standing straight and staring intently up into the hills. I got up and trotted over to her.

"What is it?"

"I saw somebody. Just a glimpse, but it was somebody dressed funny, running over the top of that hill."

"Dressed funny how?"

"Oh, in those dumb war clothes everybody wears. With the brown-and-green-and-black splotches."

"Cammies."

"What?"

"Camouflaged field uniform."

"That's it. Whoever it was must have been ducked down up there somewhere. I was trying to look all around, the way you'd been doing. All of a sudden, this apparition rose up like from out of the ground and trotted over the top of the hill."

"Standing erect?"

"No, sort of crouched over. If I hadn't been looking right at him at the time, I never would have seen him."

"Show me where, exactly."

She pointed along the car door to a slope beyond the one Nikki's body was on. It was the way a man might travel to intersect with the front road again, further back in the hills.

"He must have gotten rattled when I..." I tried to bite it off, but Allison was too smart for that.

"You found her, didn't you?"

"Yes. Just before you called. She's on the little hill behind the cabin. Somebody shot her once in the head. At least she wouldn't have suffered."

Allison stepped back and stared at me. "How can you say that? She was terrified! She knew somebody was after her. She was trying to get away and probably knew she didn't have a chance. What do you mean she wouldn't have suffered. She must have died a dozen times over before she was shot!"

I grabbed one arm and shook her a little roughly. "Allison, it's done with. We can't do anything for her now but try to make it up to her."

She jerked back her head. "You're not going after him?"

"Not now. I'll stay here. But I want you to drive back to Fernwood. Call the Monterey sheriff's office and ask for Wally Hamlin. He's a homicide detective I've worked with. Tell him about the girl and what you saw. It'll probably be too late, but tell him he might want to bring down a dog team if he can raise one, to try tracking the man who went over the hill. Tell him you'll stay at Fernwood until the first patrol unit gets there. You can lead them in."

Allison closed her eyes, took a deep breath and repeated very nearly word for word the instructions I'd just given her. Then she opened her eyes, turned and got into the car. "What are you going to be doing?" she asked, putting the car into gear.

"Just keeping an eye on things. Oh, and Allison. Do not tell Wally about the audio tapes Nikki left for me."

"I'd forgotten all about them. But why not tell him?"

"I want to listen to them first. They might involve a client of mine."

She gave me a lingering look, then took off back out to the road with the tires spitting dirt behind her. I waited until she was down the road and out of sight, then turned and started running, back behind the cabin, up the slope Nikki's body was on, over the top and across to the further, higher hill the man in cammies had gone over. I stayed below the ridgeline and worked my way thirty or forty yards past the point Allison had seen the uniformed man top the rise. I moved on up to the top and stayed low to study the territory on the other side of the hill. Other hills like the one I was on rolled on in the distance. I didn't see anybody. I stood up and walked a few paces further along the ridgeline.

I heard a little bang of some sort off in the distance, and then several hundred yards off to the right I had a glimpse of a large dark car roar across a short stretch of road just visible between two hills. It was moving fast and headed east. There must be another way to get out of there besides on the road that passed Nikki's cabin. I holstered the revolver and trotted back down, past Nikki's killing place, to pause outside the cabin and look at my watch and make a couple of notes about the estimated time of arrival, time of finding the body and Allison's spotting the person going over the ridge top. Then I walked back out to the pocket of trees the phone lines went through. From there I could see where somebody had swung up into the trees and snipped the phone wire. The severed ends dangled down through the limbs. The line must have been cut just before Nikki was chased out of her home and shot to death.

The killer must have been pursuing Nikki when she pulled into her parking place and ran for the cabin. There had to be at least two men involved in all this. One of them could have climbed the trees and cut the phone line while the other ran after Nikki. The terrified girl must have seen him coming, dropped the phone and tried to run away up the hill out back. And by that time, the man who had cut the phone line could have heard my car coming. When Allison had left, I'd been able to hear the car until I got to the top of the low hill Nikki's body was on. So the man who'd cut the phone wire could have shouted a warning to the man who was about to shoot Nikki. They could have agreed to meet further along the road. The man who cut the wire could have gotten in their car and driven off just before I arrived, while his partner killed Nikki and started over the hills.

It was the second murder in the area that had occurred just moments before somebody else came on the scene. Wally Hamlin had told me if Jo Sommers hadn't killed her husband, she must have been there almost soon enough to have seen it done. But then, you never knew what might have happened if somebody had arrived sooner. The saving of a life, or the taking of more?

I went back to the red VW. The first time I'd looked inside the car it was to find people. This time it was to find anything else worth noting. And there was something worth noting, an envelope, jammed partly behind the front seat cushion on the passenger side. It looked as if it held the stub of a utility bill. I used my knife to bend the envelope so I could see the back of it. It had a word scrawled on it. The writing was jerky, the sort a person might make trying to drive a car over rough road and at the same time, write something. There was a small pencil she might have used on the floor in front of the seat. I studied the writing for several seconds before it made any sense. As best I could tell she'd written *Radioman.* It didn't set off any bells in my head. I left the car and walked back around the cabin and up the slope, to settle down on the ground a little ways off from Nikki's body, keeping her company, waiting for the law and feeling bad about things.

Chapter 9———————

It turned out Wally Hamlin's father had died that morning over in Fresno, and Wally was on emergency leave. The lead investigator taking his place, a spare, dark, scowling man named Betta, wasn't nearly as pleasant to deal with. He had lines around his eyes as if he didn't get enough sleep nights, and he walked around with his chin thrust out. He listened to my story a couple of times, making notes that he punctuated with irritable little grunts, toured the scene and came back to ask me more questions.

"When you talked to the victim on the phone this morning, you say you asked her if whatever sort of trouble she was in could have been connected with the death of Mrs. Sommers's husband. And she told you, 'It might be'?"

"She said either, 'It might be,' or 'It might.'"

"Why the hell couldn't she be more definite about a thing like that?"

"She didn't sound all that sure about it. She sounded upset. She'd already been shaken by the Sommers killing. If she thought her own life was threatened, maybe it was just natural for her to link the two. I don't know. It's lame, I admit."

Betta snorted. He put a lot more into it than Allison does. He looked across to where men from the coroner's office were putting Nikki Scarborough's sacked-up body into their van.

"That 'radioman,'" Betta said. "That mean anything to you?"

"No. Maybe it means somebody with a local radio station. A disc jockey or engineer or time salesman or somebody."

Betta shook his head and put a stick of gum into his mouth. Chewing it gave him a chance to show off his outthrust chin.

Allison had wandered off into a field across the road. She'd told the deputies, and then Betta, what she'd seen, then gone off by herself to try to calm down.

"Lieutenant?"

We turned. One of the deputies had found a key to the shed padlock in Nikki's purse. He'd spent the past few minutes searching it.

"We got money back here," he called.

I followed Betta over to the shed. "She had a stall at the jazz festival," I told him. "Probably picked up a few bucks there. I even bought a coffee mug from her myself."

The deputy had found a stack of money with a rubber band around it. "I riffled the edges," he told Betta. "Twenties and fifties, mostly. I'd guess there's between two and three thousand dollars here all told."

Betta turned back to me, his jaw working on the gum. "How much business was she doing at the jazz festival?"

"Not that much."

The deputy slipped the money into a plastic bag. I followed Betta back around to the front of the cabin.

"Okay, Bragg," he said. "Where do you see yourself fitting into all this?"

"Not much of anywhere. She certainly wasn't a

client. I returned a phone call from her, then when she wasn't at the Fernwood cafe, I drove on out with the lady across the way to see if I could suggest a way out of whatever was troubling her. I didn't get here soon enough, and I don't know what her problem was."

"What about Mrs. Sommers?"

"She's a client. She wants me to assist you people in any way I can to find whoever killed her husband. It's a pragmatic bit of work. She's afraid she might not get the proceeds of an insurance policy if we can't show somebody else killed him."

"Assist us people? How?"

"Oh, come on, Betta. I've been in the business for a lot of years. I'll be working at it full time. Some people would talk to me who wouldn't talk to you people. I'll share what I get with you. This morning, I suggested to Nikki Scarborough that she go to the police if she felt she was in danger."

"You didn't tell me that. What did she answer?"

"She said no, she couldn't do that. She didn't say why."

"Which probably means she was involved in something she shouldn't have been," he speculated.

"Like what?"

"Like dealing in cocaine. Putting little bags of it in some of that pottery she was selling to musicians and high rollers at the festival."

"That's not bad," I admitted.

"Yeah. Maybe we'll turn up something more around here. Okay, get your lady and take off. But keep in touch."

"Sure."

The ride back up the coast was a quiet one. Allison was in a down mood, and just looked out at the passing scenery. I had too many things to think about right then to try cheering her up. And it wasn't just the killings of Dr. Haywood Sommers and Nikki Scarborough occupying my mind. I was thinking about Allison as well. I let her know what I was thinking as we approached the busy intersection of Highway 1 and Rio Road, at the south entrance to Carmel.

"I think things are going to start getting a little sticky," I told her.

She shot me a look. "I thought they began doing that Friday night."

"I mean, I'm going to be more involved. No more time for sightseeing. I'd like to put you on a plane to San Francisco. From there you can get a flight to Arcata. Our office has an account with Butler Aviation. I'll call there and fix it for you."

"No."

She was looking away from me, out the window, staring across at the expanding shopping center east of the highway. When the light changed, I turned left and drove up past Carmel Mission and headed west toward the motel.

"All right, then. You can take the car, if you want. I'll rent another. You can go home at your own pace. Stop here and there along the coast and sketch things."

She was staring straight ahead out the windshield now. She turned her head for a quick glance, then faced forward again. The movement left her long, blonde hair shimmering along the side of her face.

"No, Pete. Not this time."

"What do you mean, not this time?"

"I've been thinking about it off and on ever since you saw that newspaper Saturday, the one that told you your old girl friend was in trouble."

"She was never a girl friend."

"Whatever. You've been thinking about her and

her troubles ever since. Not every moment, but enough. So I've been thinking about us."

My stomach muscles tightened. I was afraid of what she might be trying to tell me. We had reached the small parking area on the street up behind the motel. I pulled in and turned off the motor but didn't make a move to get out.

Allison scrunched back into the corner of the seat and stared at me. "I've got to find out one way or another if I can really be this close to a man who's involved in the things that you seem to be."

"Most of my work is pretty routine."

"Two killings in four days?"

"Granted, that's not very routine."

"But it happens with you. And what I have to decide once and for all is whether I can take the fallout."

"I don't quite get that."

She stared at her hands a moment, then looked up at me. "Most of the time, at home, out in my studio, I have to think about you in kind of an abstract way. You're that fellow down in San Francisco I get together with once in a while for some of the finest moments of my life."

That touched me more than I liked. Her eyes were beginning to glisten. I reached out without thinking and grasped one of her hands. She put her other down on top of my own.

"Up there in Barracks Cove, it has to be abstract for two reasons," she told me. "One, if I think of you—us—the times we spend together, I become rather too horny to be able to concentrate on my work. And two, if I let my imagination ride along with the sort of people and things you might be encountering in the way you make your living, I'm apt to just go all to pieces inside of myself, like I was watching a slow crawl of every nightmare I've ever had since I was a little kid."

She closed her eyes a minute. When she opened them again she blinked rapidly. "Well, mister, there's not much I can do about the first, but there damn sure is one thing I'm going to try to do about the second. I'm going to stick it out with you one time— this time—while you're doing your thing. If I can live with it in person, maybe it'll help me live with it when we're a couple of hundred miles apart."

I took a deep breath. "I can't do my job and be worrying about what might happen to you, Allison. I can't have you with me every minute of the time."

"Oh goddamn it, Pete. I don't care about that. I don't even care if you take that woman to bed. But I want to be *here*, not up in Barracks Cove. In a vicarious sort of way I want to go through it with you every step of the way. I want to feel your vibrations, hear your thoughts, get your viewpoint on things when you come in at night, or at dawn, or whenever you plop down to recharge yourself. I won't be a nuisance. It's just something I have to do for once, instead of running back to Barracks Cove like a little girl to sit and fret and wait for Daddy to come home from the war."

I broke up the hand-holding and scratched my head. "I don't know if that is such a good idea."

"Why not?"

"I don't know, otherwise I'd tell you. I don't know that it's a bad idea, but I don't know that it's a good idea, either."

"I won't be any trouble."

"I'm sure you won't. In fact, it'd be kind of nice to have somebody to bounce ideas off once in a while. And, lord knows, I do like the idea of having a pretty woman waiting around the motel for when I show up."

Allison snorted. "I'm not going to be waiting around the motel all the time, and besides, I'm not the only pretty woman waiting around to see you."

"If you mean Jo Sommers, you can forget about her. She's just another client."

"Sure. I could forget about her the way I could forget about a missing hand. If it's not her, what is it? Why don't you want me around?"

"I don't know. A feeling I have."

She just looked at me a minute. "I'm my own person, Bragg," she told me. "I'm staying. If you want me to move out so you can bring her back here with you, then I'll find someplace else. But I'm hanging on the edge of this one. It's not just Jo. It's for all the times in the future there might be. When you're working and I'm up in my studio trying to maintain my sanity. That's what this is all about."

I'm usually fairly close-mouthed. I don't ordinarily shoot off words without thinking. But this was one time when feelings skipped ahead of brain. I heard myself saying, in measured tones, "I love you."

We sat for a moment without speaking, then she pulled back one fist and gave me a stinging punch to the arm. "Then let's go do something about the horny bit."

When I left the motel later, I suggested we go rent a car for Allison to use. She said she wouldn't need one. She'd walk up to town for dinner, then come back and read a book she'd brought along. It was a paperback gothic romance, about four inches thick. She said it was enough to keep her mind off things for a couple of days while I was out in the world.

I drove back down to the shopping center along Rio Road and telephoned Jo Sommers to tell her I was coming by to see her. I could have phoned her from the motel room, but I didn't see any sense in having Allison's imagination any more active than it already was.

Jo answered the door wearing a pair of taut-fitting black satin slacks and a white blouse of very thin silk. She wasn't wearing a bra beneath it, and I was reminded of some of the things that small-breasted women can get away with that larger-breasted women can't.

"You look like you're going to a party," I told her.

"Woody liked me to wear hostess outfits for the cocktail hour," she told me, closing the door and looping an arm around my own to lead me down the hallway. "It's a habit I'll probably keep up for a while. How was your day?"

"A little bleak. I'm here to tell you about it."

"All right. Let's go into Woody's study. I suppose I should feel like sealing it off, after what happened there. But I've decided I have to learn to live with it."

"Sure."

She had rearranged the furniture some. The chair her husband had been sitting in when Jo found his body was shoved over into a corner. She'd brought in some white wicker furniture from another part of the house and hung some bright travel posters on the walls in place of the battle scenes. There was a fire going in the fireplace that looked like it had been touched off about the time I'd hung up the phone at the shopping center on Rio Road.

"Would you like a drink?"

"Sure. A gin and tonic, if you have it."

"I have it." She went to another corner and slid back a door to reveal another wet bar similar to the one in the living room. Maybe they had one of those in every room of the house. She poured a couple of stiff drinks, brought mine to me and held up hers so we could clink glasses.

"Cheers," she said.

"Yeah, the same," I told her, my eyes drawn to the spot on the rug where Wally Hamlin told me her husband's body had lain about seventy-two hours earlier. It's a pleasure to witness the resiliency of the human spirit. The drink tasted mostly of gin. I put it aside to let some of the ice melt.

"Notice anything around the neighborhood today?" I asked her.

"No. It was quite typical. Like a wilderness area."

"Get any phone calls?"

She tilted her head. "Is this a part of your investigation?"

"Yes, it is."

She took a sip of her drink and crossed to sit in an easy chair she'd brought into the room from somewhere. "I had several telephone calls. From various friends and acquaintances expressing their condolences. Nothing out of the ordinary."

"Did you hear from Nikki Scarborough, by any chance?"

"I don't think so. No, I'm sure not. She's probably back down the coast. She has a little place at Big Sur. Why?"

"Some questions have come up about her background. Do you know if she uses drugs?"

Jo's shoulder moved slightly beneath the thin blouse. "She smokes a little grass from time to time. We all do."

"Anything heavier?"

"Not that I know of. I doubt it."

"Is there a possibility she could have been involved in dealing drugs? Cocaine, maybe?"

"Absolutely not." She took another sip of her drink and then held the glass off to one side. "She had a brother down in Florida somewhere who was involved in all that. He was a user himself. And a pilot. He snorted his brains away. Thought the entire world was out to get him. Somebody was still foolish enough to ask him to fly in a load of the stuff. One night, hauling a million or so dollars' worth of the white stuff, he flew into downtown Miami. Literally. In a long, shallow glide, smack into the seventh floor of a condominium."

She took another sip of the drink and settled herself more comfortably in the deep chair she was in. "Nikki is definitely anti-cocaine, Peter. She has even been so gross as to chide others who were using it at a party we both attended one time at Pebble Beach. It was during the Crosby golf thing."

"What about money matters? How well off is she?"

Again, the shoulder movement. "She manages to scrape by, like the rest of us. What is all this to do with Nikki? You needn't play detective with me, Peter. You're working for me, remember?"

"I remember. Some people from the county sheriff's office found a couple of thousand dollars stashed in her little workshop this afternoon. They were going over the place after I sent Allison to call to tell them I'd found her body on the slope behind her cabin. She'd been shot through the head."

The glass of gin and tonic slipped out of her hand onto the carpet, but she paid it no mind at all. I got up and went over to the bar and wet a towel. Jo just gaped off across the room. I picked up the ice and put it back in the glass and was mopping the rug when she turned to look down at me.

"Jesus Christ, you made that up."

"You wouldn't say that if you'd found her the way I did."

She swung back into the chair and stared straight ahead, sucking the knuckle of one hand. Sam the cat came to the study doorway to see what all the fuss was about.

"When was that?" Jo asked sharply enough to make the cat blink and back out of the room.

"This afternoon. Sometime after three."

"Why had you gone there?"

"She left a message with my answering service in San Francisco this morning. Said she was in trouble and wanted to talk to me. I got in touch with her and agreed to meet her at a little restaurant down near where she lives. She was there waiting, but then got up and left suddenly, before I arrived. I got directions to her place and drove on out. From the looks of things, she'd been shot just before I got there. Allison saw the man who probably did it going over a nearby hill at about the same time I found the body. After I sent Allison off for help, I climbed the nearby hill. I think the man who killed her got into a car that was waiting for him up the road from Nikki's place. That means at least two people were involved in the killing."

I finished doing the best I could with the rug, then went back to the bar, made her a fresh drink in a clean glass and carried it over to her. She took it without a word and drank about half of it. I sat down and took a sip of my own.

"When I talked to Nikki on the phone I asked her if her problem had anything to do with your husband's murder. She wasn't sure but indicated there might have been a connection. After they found the money, the sheriff's people thought she might have been dealing in drugs. So what do you think about all that?"

Jo looked a little out of it. It was several moments before she came back from wherever she'd been and stared at me blankly. Then she had another drink of her drink, which pretty well finished it, and got up and went across to fix herself another. She came back and sat down, hunching forward and staring at me with all the sincerity she could muster. "I don't know what to think."

"Jo, you're not leveling with me. Her killing was a shock, but you know she was mixed up in something. What was it?"

"Peter, I swear, I don't know. But if she said it had something to do with my husband...Well, she knew Woody, of course. And they seemed affectionate toward one another, despite the difference in their ages."

I hoisted my eyebrows a ways.

"Oh, I don't mean they were lovers, though they could have been, so far as I know. They were fond of each other. Nikki did quite a handsome sculpture of Woody's head one time. It's over there, atop the bookcase."

I got up and strolled over to where she pointed. I'd seen a couple of framed photos of the late doctor when I'd gone through the house on Saturday, so I had something with which to compare the rendition of a man's head in rust-colored modeling clay atop the bookcase. It could have been Sommers or somebody living up the street. But then, I don't know how hard something like that might be. I went back to my chair and had another sip of the drink.

"They were fond of each other," I repeated.

"Yes, and...Oh, I don't know, sometimes I had the feeling they were talking about things they didn't want me to know about."

She was winging it, I felt, but she was beginning to warm up to it pretty well.

"I mean, Nikki would come visit sometimes, you know, and I'd be doing things around the house. She could come in here to chat with Woody, and sometimes their voices would drop, and I'd know they were talking about something they didn't want me to overhear. It didn't bother me, really. They were like a couple of kids together."

"Were there phone calls between them?"

"Of course. Nikki would call, and if I answered we'd talk for a few moments, then sometimes she'd ask to speak with my husband. And, of course, there's a phone over on the desk. Woody could have called her at any time. We tried to respect the privacy of each other's phone conversations."

I grunted. "Allison and I were at a party Saturday evening. We met a personable young fellow working as a bartender there, who also works at a bar called the Duck's Quack in town. Allison and I went by there the next evening and saw him in conversation with Nikki. Alex something his name was."

Her face brightened. "Oh, of course. Alex Kilduff. He's a very popular young man. That's why he's asked to work so many private parties. Everybody seems to know him."

"Did he and Nikki go together?"

"I don't know. They might have, at least some of the time. Nikki mentions him—used to mention him—in conversation from time to time. But I doubt if there was any steadfast relationship between them. Alex goes with a lot of women. How is Allison, by the way. Is she still here?"

"Yeah, she plans to stick around for a few more days. She's fine. Probably would have sent her regards if she'd known I'd be by to see you."

"Oh. Well, you must be sure to say hello to her for me. But Peter...I mean, it's terrible, what happened to Nikki, but why are you asking so many questions about her? Aren't you trying to find my husband's killer?"

Her concentration was beginning to zig and zag. "Yes, I am. But if your husband and Nikki had some sort of relationship and both of them are killed within a matter of days, I'd be foolish to ignore the possibility that their deaths are related somehow." I had another sip of the drink. "When I came here the other day to feed the cat, the sheriff's investigator told me something about a tape recorder that was on your husband's desk."

She sat up a little straighter. "We have two recorders. A desk model Woody used in his practice, and a little portable."

"Could I use one of them? I have a couple of tapes I'd like to listen to."

"All right. Which of them would you like?"

"Doesn't matter."

She got up and walked over to the desk in the far corner. She brought a small tape recorder over to me but didn't go back to her chair immediately.

"Peter, did the sheriff's people tell you about a tape they found on this, after my husband's murder?"

"Yes, they did."

She returned to her chair and reached for the gin and tonic, giving me a little smile. "It wasn't as serious as they tried to make out," she told me. "With Woody, it was like some sort of game. He'd hide the recorder somewhere and turn it on, then get me in here and goad me into an argument. He would play it back for me sometime later. Sometimes during an intimate moment. He thought it was great fun, and I got used to it after a while. In fact, I got so I rather liked it. It gave me an excuse to go out and find a younger man to flirt with. That particular night, on Friday, I found you, at the jazz festival. But the sheriff's people couldn't understand that."

"I suppose they couldn't. They told me your husband threatened to toss you out."

"He did that, but he never meant it."

"Why not?"

"Because he was a man by now somewhat in decline compared to what he was when we met and married. He knew full well he'd never find a woman as young as I am again, who would put up with living with him. As young as I am, and, I might as well add, as artful about some things as I am."

"You maintained a decent physical relationship to the end, then?"

"Decent is putting it mildly. He was a vigorous man, to the end, as you say. And he used to call me the best fuck in the continental United States." She had another sip of the drink. "I took that as quite a compliment. He traveled extensively, you know." She was staring at me with a blank face.

I cleared my throat, then took out one of the tapes Nikki Scarborough had left for me at the Fernwood cafe and put it into the recorder. I hit the play button.

From the recorder came the sound of a man harrumphing a couple of times, then saying, *"One, two, three, four, here we go..."*

Jo bolted out of her chair, nearly dropping her drink again. She had a stricken look on her face. I hit the stop button.

"What's wrong?"

"That's Woody's voice. It's the little prologue he went through, whenever taping a patient. Where did you get it?"

"I'll come to that. Did your husband tape all the sessions he had with his patients?"

"Most of them. Unless the patient was adamantly opposed. At those times he took thorough notes and would transcribe those to tape as soon as the session ended and the patient had left. Where did you get it, Peter?"

"Nikki left this and another tape for me at the cafe we were supposed to meet at in Big Sur. Did your husband keep all the tapes from his days of practice?"

"Yes. Most of them are in a storage loft in the garage. Where would Nikki have gotten her hands on it?"

"That's what I was going to ask you. Let's hear what's on it, before the sheriff's people come by."

"Sheriff's people? Coming here again?"

"Somebody's bound to eventually, to ask you about Nikki. I had to tell them the two of you knew each other."

"Why did you have to tell them that?"

"Jo, when you're the person who finds a body and reports it to the cops, you have to tell them pretty much everything you know about it, if you don't want to take that solemn ride into the lockup. Now pipe down a minute, I want to hear this."

I started the recorder again. Jo got up and went across to the bar to fix herself another drink. The gin didn't seem to be having much effect on her. The doctor's voice continued:

"August 1977. La Jolla, California. We are exploring the dilemma that presented itself during the closing days of the American presence in Vietnam. You were at the loading bay of the cargo plane at Danang airport. The woman and your child were in the mob of people being held back at the perimeter of the loading area. Your aircraft is at, or near, capacity. You can hear the rumble of distant shellfire. Enemy troops are advancing, friendly troops are retreating.

"Now, we are going to force ourselves to analyze each of these conditions in turn. You at the plane. The woman and child in the throng. The approaching fighting. We are going to explore what options were realistically open to you, and rate each of these options as to their probability, or capability, of success. . . ."

I didn't know where he was going with this, but the doctor seemed to know his business. At least it made sense to me to separate out different elements of an awful experience.

I flipped the recorder switch to fast forward. When I put it back on listening speed, the doctor and his patient, a man with a low-pitched, agitated voice, were discussing the man's relationship with the woman. I didn't know the patient, but I didn't feel as if I had the right to listen in on any more of his woes. I flipped the cassette to play the other side.

"Did the doctor see his patients for hour-long sessions?"

"Not quite. He told me once he tried to hold them to fifty minutes. Then, after the patient left, he would voice his evaluation of the session, and what direction he might go during the next visit by the same patient."

I ran the recorder on fast forward again to near the end of the tape. "Did he discuss his work with you much?"

"No, not much. Just in the way other men might come home and tell their wives about a funny thing that happened at the office that day."

I couldn't tell if she was making a little joke or what. Her nose was back into her gin and tonic.

Toward the end of the tape I put it on play again. The patient had evidently left, and Sommers was recording his evaluation of the session. During the time I listened, he used a lot of jargon I didn't understand, then mentioned the patient's name a couple of times. A chap named Bergman.

I changed tapes to listen to the second one Nikki had left for me. I ran it fast forward, then stopped it randomly somewhere near the middle of the first side. The man speaking was another patient. He had a flat, almost artificial-sounding voice. He was talking about an ambulance ride he'd had somewhere.

"It occurred to me at the time how fitting it was that I should be leaving the field in an ambulance, for a very great

part of me felt as if it had died. At least . . . At least I knew I had left my soul back there. . . ."

I stopped the tape and put the recorder on fast forward. I wondered how a man could spend a professional lifetime dealing with this sort of thing. I flipped the tape to play the other side. Jo was back over at the bar, pouring more mirth into her glass. Maybe she got it from her late husband. I think with the stories he'd had to listen to and deal with for a lifetime, it wouldn't be unusual if the man had stayed drunk for the duration of his retirement.

When I put the recorder on play once again the doctor was giving his sum-up. And when he mentioned the patient's name I sat up straight. It was Wakefield, and I thought of the brightly lighted home on the hill overlooking the Carmel Valley, and the host of the Saturday night party, a man in the uniform of an army major general.

Chapter 10 —————————

Gus Wakefield had a smile in his voice when I first phoned, but that changed soon after I explained that Mrs. Sommers had hired me to find her husband's killer and added that I'd come upon something that indicated he might be of assistance. I told him I'd like to drive out to see him.

"If it's a minor point, maybe we could clear it up on the telephone," he suggested.

"I would say, sir, it's more in the realm of a major point, which combined with something you told me the other evening makes me think we really should sit down together and talk things over."

He took his time about it but seemed to come to the conclusion it wouldn't accomplish much trying to stall me. I guess if you've made major general, you're capable of making the nasty decisions and acting on them.

"All right. Why don't you come now? I can see you before dinner."

The shadows were lengthening in the Valley when I got to the road that meandered up the hillside toward the Wakefield home.

The general answered the door himself with a brusque greeting and led me through the large room where the party had been held over the weekend. The rugs and furniture were back in place, turning it into just another mammoth living room with a spectacular view.

Beyond the living room was a hallway with a bathroom off one side and a small study off the other. The study had a desk, a couple of chairs, photos and memorabilia on the walls and the view of the Valley. Wakefield, wearing gray slacks, a white sports shirt and an argyle-patterned, gray-and-blue pullover sweater, gestured toward one of the chairs and settled into the swivel chair at the desk.

"I'm not going to go through the civility of offering you a drink, Mr. Bragg. If we're going to talk about murder, I'd rather have all my senses about me."

We weren't on a first-name basis any longer.

"No offense, Mr. Wakefield, I feel the same way. Or would you prefer to be called general?"

"Under the circumstances, just Wakefield should be adequate. Please get to the point."

"All right. This afternoon I came into possession of a pair of audio tape cassettes. Just before phoning you, I played portions of them. They apparently were tapes that had been recorded by Dr. Sommers when he was in practice. They were of sessions with his patients, followed by summations of those sessions by the doctor after the patient had left. I didn't feel right about listening in on them. He was speaking to troubled men. But I felt I needed to get some idea of what these tapes were about, because of the unusual circumstances under which they came into my possession. The first tape didn't mean much to me. But during the summary of the second one, Dr. Sommers mentioned your name. And the brief portion of the conversation between Dr. Sommers and the patient mentioned an ambulance ride."

Wakefield got up out of his chair and went to stare out the windows, his hands clasped tightly behind his back. I didn't know if it was pay dirt, but I'd hit something.

"Then I recalled at the party the other evening, sir, you said something about—how Dr. Sommers could have caused a lot of mischief in this community, if he were of a mind to. How he could trigger intolerable memories in some of his former patients. Some of whom might even live in the Monterey area. Were you one of his patients, sir?"

He continued standing with his back to me for several moments more, then turned and dropped back into the chair. He looked like a different man— depleted and chalky-faced. When he raised his eyes, there was appeal in them.

"I appreciate that you have a job to do, Mr. Bragg. I, on the other hand, have no further job to do. I'm supposed to be relaxing and enjoying the sunset years, after a career of service to my country. I don't much like the idea that somebody else's job must now intrude in my own life."

We just stared at each other. There was nothing I could say, really. I didn't blame him for the way he felt. He turned, finally, and pressed a key on an internal communications unit I hadn't noticed in a bookcase alongside the desk. A woman's voice answered. I recognized it as his wife's.

"Dear, something important has come up. I might have to beg off dinner for a bit."

Their conversation was muted and brief. He switched off the device and turned back to me. "Mr. Bragg, what I have to tell you, I haven't told to another person living in this area. I would prefer to have it remain that way, so far as it is within your discretion."

"You have my word, sir."

"Good. Then to answer your question, no, I was not a patient of Woody Sommers. But my brother

Hadley was. In fact, I'm the one who arranged for Woody to try helping my brother. Dr. Sommers and I had met some while before, when we were both serving at the Pentagon. I am only going to give you the essential details of this, Mr. Bragg. And then, in turn, I would like to know how you came into possession of that recording."

"Fair enough."

"My younger brother was a fresh second lieutenant with a rifle company in Korea. His group was on the line for sixteen days solid, battling over one of those interminable hills in that godforsaken country. It was the first combat for Hadley and most of the other men. Green outfits weren't ordinarily thrown into that sort of situation, but our troops were being rather chewed up right then. They were there out of necessity."

He closed his eyes for the time it took him to take a deep breath and let it back out. "Hadley cracked. Under fire. Pure and simple. He just left the position and walked away. When he got to an area in back of the fighting, he went up to an aid station and commandeered a vehicle at gunpoint. That was the ambulance mentioned on that tape. He had himself driven to a regimental command post and reported to a senior officer. He told the people there he'd deserted his position and that he wasn't going back there, no matter the cost. He was shipped home under guard and held at a disciplinary barracks at Fort Lewis, Washington, pending court-martial. When I learned of it, I managed for Woody Sommers to fly out to see him. I'm not quite sure what I hoped for. Something that might put my brother's heart back together, maybe. Something that might assist his defense. Something that might explain what had happened to him. I didn't know then and I don't know to this day. It hardly mattered. He might well have been shot before a firing squad for what he did.

"Woody had three sessions with Hadley, over a five-day period. On the night following the third session, my brother hanged himself from a water pipe traversing the barracks ceiling."

He looked at me coldly but in full control of himself. Maybe he didn't talk about it to anybody, but he'd grown to live with it long ago.

"I'm sorry," I told him.

He just grunted. "Where did you get the recording?"

"It, along with another, was left for me at a small restaurant down in Big Sur, by a woman potter named Nikki Scarborough. Do you know her by any chance?"

"No, the name means nothing to me."

"I met her a few days ago through a mutual friend. She learned what sort of work I do, and this morning we talked on the telephone. She wanted to see me about some sort of trouble she said she was in. We agreed to meet at the restaurant, but she left there just before I arrived. But she had left the tapes behind for me."

"I would like to speak to this woman."

"Yes, well, she's dead, Mr. Wakefield. I got directions to where she lived and drove on out there. Somebody had shot her just a short time before I arrived."

Gus Wakefield sat back in his chair, his face rigid.

"I phoned the sheriff's office and went over things with the investigators, but I didn't tell them about the tapes, and I don't intend to, unless it turns out that's the only way to find whoever killed the young woman. The sheriff probably could have my license lifted if he learned I had the tapes and didn't tell his men about them, but I think you're a man of honor and that you'd just as soon have them kept out of circulation yourself. And I guess the reason I'm telling you all this is with the hope that now you'll tell me anything else you might know about what's been going on around here."

"You think Woody's death, and now the girl's, are related?"

"The tapes make it look that way. The sheriff's investigators seemed to think the girl might have been dealing in narcotics, because of some money that was found out at her place. I tend to think something else is behind all of it."

He took his time about replying. He turned in his chair and looked out the window some. "I knew this recording existed before you told me about it, Mr. Bragg. Somebody sent me a copy of it, Woody's session with Hadley. About a month ago. Somebody else thought, as you did, that the Wakefield mentioned on the tape was myself. There was a note with it informing me I would be receiving a telephone call in connection with it. Two days later, I did receive such a call. The caller spoke in a muffled, deep voice. He asked—I assume it was a man—he asked for a one-time payment of ten thousand dollars. He said if I didn't pay, he would mail other copies of the same tape to various people I know. To the *Monterey Herald*. To a local radio station which has a rather sensational format. To the secretary of a golf club I belong to. The *Monterey Herald*, I'm sure, wouldn't have touched something like that with a ten-foot pole. The person on the phone was just trying to create a climate of fear. But I just laughed at him. Or rather, I feigned a laugh. That was the tack I had decided to take when I received the promised phone call. I told the caller it was my brother on the tape, not myself, and that Hadley had been dead for thirty years. Then I hung up. I never heard from him again."

"Did you go to the police?"

"To what end? No, I didn't go to the police. Any more than I would be inclined to go to them now, about the copy this woman left for you. The error of my brother wouldn't affect my standing or reputation in the community, but then—it isn't the sort of family failing one easily laughs off, either."

"Did you talk to Dr. Sommers about it?"

"No. Why? You think if I had he might be alive now?"

"Not at all. I just thought you might have been curious about how one of his tapes fell into other hands."

"I didn't even know the tape was his. It could have been army property, for all I knew. Dr. Sommers obviously wouldn't have been the one to send it to me, since he knew it concerned not me but my brother. No, I just didn't see any purpose in mentioning it to anybody."

"Since that phone call, have you speculated about who might have done it?"

"Of course. A thing like that isn't easily dismissed. Jo Sommers came to mind, of course, but I doubted it was her. One would think she would be more sure of her target. I think she would have found out from Woody that I wasn't the person on the tape."

"Have you heard of anybody else in the area who might have received one of Dr. Sommers's tapes, along with a follow-up extortion call?"

He hesitated just long enough to color his reply. "No, I haven't. Do you think that's why he was killed, then? Somebody thought he was trying to extort money from them?"

"It's the only thing that's turned up so far."

"And this woman who was killed today. Since she had two of the tapes, you think her death might have been for the same reason?"

"Maybe."

"I was a fool," he said quietly. "I should have talked to Woody about this."

"But you're sure, sir, you don't know anybody else, either here or in some other part of the country, who might have been sent one of the recordings?"

He got up out of his chair. "No, I do not. And now, Mr. Bragg, you'll have to excuse me. I've told you everything I know about the matter."

I drove back out of the Valley and pulled into a service station near Highway 1 to use a pay phone. I looked up Billy Carpenter's number and dialed it. His wife told me he was back out at the fairgrounds, finishing up business to do with the weekend jazz festival. I called around out there and finally found him at the Hunt Club. I told him I wanted to pick his brains, and he said to join him; so I drove over the hill to the fairgrounds and Hunt Club. Billy was at the bar sipping a Scotch and water. I ordered a cup of coffee, and we went to a table off in a corner.

He was still wearing his silver 25th Anniversary Jazz Festival golf cap, along with a pair of yellow pants, a pink polo shirt and a white windbreaker.

"What's up?" he asked.

Billy and I have known each other ever since I used to work for the *Chronicle*. I dove right in. "I have a tough request. I might have a handle on the reason Doc Sommers was killed. It's possible somebody thought Doc was trying to extort money from them. Somebody did try to extort money from at least one person around here. The extortionist wasn't Sommers, but it was somebody using some compromising information Sommers had tape recorded during his psychiatric career. It involved a military matter. Then, there was a young woman murdered down in Big Sur this afternoon. She had some of this same information and might have been a part of the extortion plot. She wanted to talk to me about something, but she was dead before I caught up with her."

Billy Carpenter blinked at me, emptied the Scotch and signaled the cocktail waitress for another. "Jesus Christ," he said quietly.

"The tough request is, can you give me the name or names of anybody else around here who might have been approached in the same manner. Somebody who might have some dark corner in their past, and who was threatened with having that darkness tossed on the table for everyone to look at."

I had to wait a little too long for his reply. "You've heard something, haven't you, William?"

"Oh, yeah, but jeez, Pete. This is tough, like you said. Are you sure this is the reason Sommers was killed?"

"No, of course not. But the sheriff and D.A. might think so."

"Not Thackery," Billy said quietly.

The waitress brought him his fresh Scotch. I paid for it. "Why not Thackery?"

"He's sort of one of the, oh, group, you might say."

"What group?"

"You know. That clique of people you find anywhere. The network. The people who count. Who play golf together and do business together and arrange things the way they think things should be arranged. Around here it's various community figures and any number of people who are retired military."

"Wait a minute. You're telling me Thackery might want to tag Jo Sommers for her husband's death just to protect somebody in this clique of community-spirited citizens?"

"I didn't exactly say that."

"No, you didn't exactly. Okay, forget about Thackery.

But you have heard something about extortion and Sommers."

"Merely a whisper. A hint. A cryptic suggestion on a seventeenth fairway one day."

"And a name to go with it."

"And a name to go with it," he admitted.

"When you heard that somebody had scragged the good doctor, didn't it ring any bells inside that quick newsie's mind of yours?"

"Honestly, it didn't, Pete. Okay, here's what happened. I heard this rumor, like I said."

"What was the rumor?"

"That a certain individual who one time had consulted Woody Sommers in a professional capacity, had received an anonymous message saying if he didn't pony up five grand, certain information of a dubious nature in his background would be plastered all over the greater Monterey Bay area to the individual's acute embarrassment. The second part of the rumor was that the information in this individual's background had prompted the consultation in the past with Doc Sommers. That was the whole of it."

"Did it go anywhere from there?"

"After much anguish and indecision, I myself went somewhere from there with it. I went out to the Sommers home and told Doc about the rumor I'd heard, and point-blank asked him if he was behind it."

"What did he say?"

"He damn near threw me out on my ear. I've never seen a man so angry. He finally cooled off and brought out the bottle and we talked about it some. He said because of the nature of the incident in that particular individual's background, there would have been dozens of people who knew about it. It also was a service-connected event. The odds were pretty good that somebody who was familiar with the event in the past might know somebody living in this area and could have passed along that particularly nasty bit of information to the local party."

"But did he admit he had that same information on tape?"

"Yes, but he said he had a coding system that would keep anybody from telling what tape might be associated with any given patient. Anyway, he was convincing enough about the information not having come from him that I never even thought about the golf course rumor again, until you brought it up just now."

He was quiet for a moment. "To tell you the truth, what did cross my mind was that somebody might have whacked out Doc Sommers because of those models he has on the fireplace mantel in his den."

"I remember seeing those. What's wrong with them?"

"They're related to patient problems he's had in the past. He told me one time they represent some of his biggest wins and biggest failures during his career. You remember seeing the one of a machine gun? With its barrel pointed toward the ground?"

"Yes."

"That represents an incident in the life of a man who now is in a position of prominence with the current adminstration in Washington. The man had been a young marine on Guadalcanal in World War Two. He and a couple of other boys were manning a machine-gun position near a river crossing on a night the Japanese launched a big attack. They killed a lot of the enemy, but eventually the position was overrun. His two buddies were killed, but the patient squirmed beneath their bodies and lay doggo. He survived by staying that way for the rest of the night and the whole next day. He extricated himself from the other bodies after dark the following night and made his way back to his unit. He was never able to sleep for more than twenty minutes at a time, after that, until Woody went to work on him. Sort of made him a whole man again.

"Well, that's what those models are all about," Billy continued. "Those were the patients he used to think about in later years. He said that putting the models together helped exorcise his own mind of some of the raw memories of what those various men had been through. Which, I'm sure, is all he meant by them. Only Jesus Christ, he should have put them away in a box somewhere, when he had people over."

"Why's that?"

"Some of those models represent trauma that was suffered by men now living here, that's why. He told me so. And I had to ask myself one time. Can you imagine what it would be like to pop into the den at the Doc Sommers's place for a friendly drink, and see there on the fireplace mantel a depiction of something connected with the most traumatic experience of your life?"

Chapter 11 ——————

Billy finally gave me the name of the man who'd been whispered about on the seventeenth fairway of one of the local golf courses. I practically had to get down on my knees and make the sign of the cross while vowing I wouldn't disclose my source, but in the end he gave me the name. It was Lawrence Pitt, one of the men he'd introduced me to at the Hunt Club Friday night, and one of the men in a navy uniform I'd seen at the Wakefield party on Saturday. Wakefield had told me he'd been a destroyer skipper. Billy also gave me his address. It was back over in Carmel, in that neighborhood of well-appointed residences not far from the General Stilwell home. I didn't know if I'd catch Pitt in, but I decided to drive on over and arrive on his doorstep cold. I figured a frontal assault was the only way I might get the information from him that I needed. I didn't want to phone ahead and have him wondering about what I was after.

The yard of his home was bordered by a six-foot-high fence of redwood that over the years had weathered to gray. He had a broad front yard of well-tended grass and neatly trimmed shrubbery. The house itself had a wooden shiplap exterior painted a light tan color with black trim. A garage big enough for a couple of large cars was attached to the house.

Pitt himself answered my ring. He was wearing blue jogging pants and a white T-shirt. I hadn't noticed his barrel chest before. He looked like a tough little Popeye-the-sailor-man, only with a crewcut. He recognized me, but I still reminded him who I was and where we'd met. He didn't make any sweeping, welcoming gesture. He stood his ground at the partially open front door.

"At the request of Mrs. Sommers, I'm working with the Monterey sheriff's office on her husband's death," I told him. "From conversations I've had with other people, I believe you might be able to help me out some. I know it's an awkward time to call on you, but if you could spare me a few minutes, I'd appreciate it."

He didn't budge. You'd think I was an encyclopedia salesman.

"How could I help?" he wanted to know.

I glanced off left and right, as if the neighborhood had ears. Most neighborhoods do. "It would be better if we had a bit of privacy, sir. If you don't want me in your house, maybe you could come sit in my car for a couple of minutes."

He finally relented and opened the door. I stepped inside and glanced around. This was a family home. Comfortable, warm and cheerful. Family pictures on the walls. Books and magazines scattered about. He pointed me toward a sofa upholstered with a brown-and-yellow-patterned material. He sat in a well-used leather chair nearby.

"We won't be disturbing anybody?" I asked.

"Only me," he said with a little bristle to it. "Everybody else is out for the evening."

I cleared my throat and leaped right in. "I have spoken to two people today who told me somebody in this area has had access to information imparted to Dr. Sommers during his professional psychiatric career. I have been told this information has been used in extortion attempts on various other persons who live in the area. This information apparently was gleaned from private tape recordings Dr. Sommers made in the course of his work."

Pitt was on his feet. "Get out."

I got up reluctantly. "Please hear me out, sir. There was a young woman living at Big Sur who..."

He didn't want to hear about it. I could tell that when he threw a quick jab at my chin. He had a short reach, and I was able to see it coming in time to pop back my head and avoid the worst of it, but his knuckles glanced off my lower lip and drew a little blood. I took a backward step toward the door, but then braced myself with my hands raised, so he knew if he came at me again he could expect some resistance. Maybe a broken lamp or two and some knocked-about furniture.

"There was a young woman living at Big Sur I think might have been a part of all this who was shot through the head this afternoon," I continued.

He hadn't decided on his next move yet, but that took some of the wind out of him.

"Her name was Nikki Scarborough, and this last weekend she had a pottery stall at the jazz festival. She talked to me earlier today by phone. She was frightened and wanted to see me. By the time I got to her she was dead."

He was staring at me with his mouth in a circle like he was getting ready to whistle.

"Did you know her?" I asked.

"No. No, I didn't. But I knew who she was. Is she the one you wanted to ask me about?"

"No, sir. I'm afraid not."

His eyes flared briefly, but then he accepted it.

"I'm sorry for swinging at you," he told me. "Sit back down."

I went back to the sofa. "I might have done the same, in your position," I told him. "This is an ugly bit of business I've found myself in. I don't want to cause anybody unnecessary pain, but I do want to find out who killed Dr. Sommers. I think there's a good chance the same person killed the woman today. I think there's a good chance there might be more killings. You might be able to help me prevent that."

"How?" He was back in the leather chair.

"If you have the stomach to kill somebody, and only need a motive, extortion might do. It might be the reason somebody killed Dr. Sommers Friday night, and that girl this afternoon. Earlier today I spoke with a man who was one of the intended extortion victims. I spoke to another man who had heard a rumor about these extortion attempts, weeks ago. He had dismissed them since then for what they were, just rumors. But your name, Mr. Pitt, was a part of the rumor. And if somebody did make contact with you in an extortion attempt, successful or not, I would like to hear about it. I don't want to know about your past, or what might have made anybody think there was something you'd done that you'd like to keep buried. I'm interested only in the mechanics of any extoriton attempt. How they got in touch with you. What they told you to do. What you did do, in return."

We just stared at each other while he made up his mind.

"What if I told you?" he asked. "You said you were working with the sheriff's office. You'd have to share your information with them, wouldn't you?"

"Not unless you're the one who's been killing people around here."

"I did not kill Dr. Sommers," he said quietly. "And I certainly did not kill that girl this afternoon. But I still don't know you well enough to trust you not to share anything I might tell you with the sheriff or the local newspaper or anybody else who might strike your fancy."

"I'm a stranger," I acknowledged. "But something else I am as well is, I'm a pretty good private investigator. And the only way you get to be a pretty good private cop is by learning when to talk and when to keep your mouth shut. I figure this is one of the times to keep my mouth shut, until I find the killer, no matter what the Department of Consumer Affairs might think."

"Consumer Affairs? What do they have to do with anything?"

"In this state, they're the ones who hand out P.I. licenses."

It astonished him. He even honked out a little laugh. "You're pulling my leg."

"No sir. The California Department of Consumer Affairs. They license everybody. Private eyes, barbers, accountants. You name it, they license it."

"That's the silliest thing I ever heard of."

"It strikes me that way once in a while, too. It lightens things just enough so I figure I don't have to go blab everything I learn to the local cops. My word is good, Mr. Pitt. I could give you references, if we had the time for that sort of thing."

He made another little chuckle. "All right, Mr. Bragg. Yes, I was one of the extortion victims. Not that what I did was really of such a devastating nature. Faulty judgment while in a command position is what it was. Woody Sommers knew about it. I had maybe three or four sessions with him, is all. He was able to set my thinking straight for me. A couple of men died aboard my ship because of that judgmental error. But Woody was able to show me how half a dozen other factors could have played a part in their deaths as well."

I nodded. "I should think a certain amount of death and damage was to be expected in a war situation. It was in mine."

"Oh, sure it is. But not everybody can accept that as easily as some others might. But Doc Sommers managed to ease me over all that. It wouldn't kill me to have people learn about it now, but it might cause a certain discomfort to my family. And the amount of money they got out of me was a fair enough price, I figured, to avoid all that. I made it plain to them there would be no more of it in the future. I even tried to arrange it in such a way that I might find out who was behind it, in case anybody else I knew fell victim to the same sleazy operation."

"I'd still like to hear about the mechanics of it."

He slapped one hand on the arm of his chair. "Why not? So long as the Department of Consumer Affairs has given you a clean bill of health." He got out of the chair, chuckling again. You never knew what would win over a man.

"How about a drink?"

"Sure. Gin and tonic if you have it."

"I have it. Wait here." He went out back to the kitchen. I heard the refrigerator door open and shut and the rattle of ice. A moment later he brought in a gin and tonic for me and what looked like Scotch for him. He went back to his chair and told me about it.

"It was back in late July. Got a call here around eight o'clock one night. My daughter, Stacy, answered it and told me it was for me. When I asked her about it later, Stacy said the caller had a normal-sounding voice when she talked to him. A man. She even said she might have heard that voice before, but she couldn't be sure. Anyway, when I got to the phone, the voice was all muffled and distorted. Somebody obviously trying to disguise it. What he said was, 'Angel and Torrence. October 4, 1944. That is a two-thousand dollar mistake. Have that amount of money ready at this same time tomorrow night. Have it in a sealed manila envelope. You will receive another phone call.' And then he hung up. Angel and Torrence were the two men killed on my ship, at least partially because of an error I made."

"And you did what he asked?"

"Yes, after thinking about it for a while. And I put a little note in with the money. I told whoever it was that they were right, it had been a two-thousand dollar mistake, and that was all. They'd get no more. He didn't call the next night until nearly ten o'clock. The man with the same faked voice told me to take the money to a pay phone next to a supermarket at the Barnyard. Know where that is?"

I nodded. It was another collection of shops and restaurants a couple of blocks north of the Crossroads shopping area at Rio Road and Highway 1.

"So I drove on over there. It's only about a five-minute drive from here. When I got there, a woman was on the phone, but she hung up almost as soon as I got out of my car. I went over and the phone rang almost immediately. The same voice told me to drive next into the main business district here in Carmel. Sent me to another pay phone, on Ocean Avenue. When I got there, same as before, the phone rang. I obviously was being watched. Maybe by the man doing the calling, maybe by somebody in cahoots with him. This time, the man told me to walk up San Carlos to the Hog's Breath, that bar and restaurant owned by the movie fellow."

"Clint Eastwood. I know the place."

"He told me to go down and sit at one of the tables at the very back of the patio area, near one of those gas-fired heaters. You know where I mean? It's kind of private back there."

"I know."

"He told me to order a drink and to spend about five minutes sipping it, then to leave the envelope underneath my seat and to get up and leave. I did what he said, then I spent about an hour parked further up San Carlos, watching people come in and out of the place, but I finally realized what a foolish venture that was. I didn't know who I was looking for. Didn't know if they had an accomplice to make the pickup. Anyway, I drove on back home then, fended off questions from my wife, swore I wasn't having a flaming affair with another woman, and that was the end of it."

"He never did get in touch with you again?"

"No, sir. Wouldn't have mattered if he had. I would have ignored him."

"Was there anybody else sitting in that back patio area while you were there?"

"No. If there had been, I would have stopped them on their way out of there and asked if they'd seen anybody pick up that manila envelope."

I thought it over.

"Does that help you any?" he wanted to know.

"It tells me somebody had thought things out pretty carefully."

"That's what I decided. And I don't even have a license from the Department of Consumer Affairs."

"Were there many people around the Barnyard when you went to the phone by the supermarket?"

"Nope. Oh, there were a few people coming and going. There's a couple of restaurants still open at that time of night. But there wasn't a lot of foot traffic."

"The woman who was on the phone when you got there. Is she anybody you might have seen before?"

"I didn't recognize her. Didn't pay that much attention, to tell you the truth. It wasn't until later it occurred to me she might have been a part of it. Keeping the phone away from anybody else until I showed up."

"Would you know her if you saw her again?"

"No, I decided I wouldn't. Decided that just last weekend."

"What happened last weekend?"

"A friend of mine had the same sort of thing happen to him."

"Extortion?"

"Yes. I'm not going to tell you who he is. But we're good enough friends so he told me about it. He came up to me one day last week with a sort of sheepish grin on his face and said, 'You know, Larry, I've got a secret, and I have to figure out if it's a three-thousand dollar secret.' Well, I guessed what was going on immediately. Three-thousand dollar secret sounded painfully similar to the two-thousand dollar mistake my mystery caller had referred to back in July. So I came right out and told my friend what my experience had been. He was grateful that I told him, and I'd been right. He was being hit up the same way. And he decided that so long as I hadn't been asked for any more money after that first time, that he'd go along with it as well."

"Didn't it ever occur to you somebody might just be trying to build that sort of reputation? To leave everybody alone after the initial payoff, until he'd been through whatever list of people he had, before going back and starting all over again?"

"No," he said soberly. "That hadn't occurred to me."

"What were your friend's instructions?"

"He was told to put the money in an envelope, just like me, and to take it with him to the jazz festival

Friday night. He was told to be in the bar of the Hunt Club at a certain hour."

"The caller knew he'd be at the festival and would have access to the Hunt Club?"

"Yes, but that wasn't so unusual, if the caller knew anything about us. And he certainly knew something about our past, at least. My friend and I and a gang of other people have been going to the jazz festival for years, doing volunteer work in connection with it. That buys us a ticket to the Hunt Club, as well."

"So what happened in the Hunt Club?"

"He got a phone call at the bar. He was told to go immediately out onto the fairway there and to make a purchase at the pottery stall and to ask the woman working at the stall to hold his purchase until later, when either he or a friend would be by to pick it up. And he was to ask the woman to put the manila envelope into the bag along with the purchase. The woman at the pottery stall, of course, was that Nikki Scarborough person. About a half hour after my friend did what he was told, he got around to telling me about it. I told him he should have let me know immediately. I left the arena and watched the pottery stall from some ways off for ten or twenty minutes. But I finally decided we probably were too late. I went over to the stall and asked the woman there about it. She told me that yes, somebody had picked up that particular purchase almost immediately after. Said it was an older man. Somebody she didn't know. We talked a few minutes and I got one of her business cards. That's how I learned her name. I thought at the time she was an innocent party in it all. But after what you told me happened today, maybe she was the pickup person all along."

"Maybe. Do you have any other reason to think so?"

"I'm not just sure, that's the aggravating part of it.

You see, it crossed my mind when I went over and spoke to her Friday night, that she could have been the woman on the telephone at the Barnyard, that night back in July. Can't be sure, because I didn't make any big deal of noting what the woman on the phone looked like. But there was something about her posture. Kind of a slouch around the shoulders. It could have been the same woman, but I'm not positive."

I finished my drink and got up to go, thanking him for his help. "One other thing," I said at the door. "You said you won't tell me your friend's name. Will you tell me if he was there at the Hunt Club when I stopped in with Mrs. Sommers Friday night, and Billy Carpenter introduced us all?"

"No, Mr. Bragg, I won't even tell you that. But you shouldn't spend so much time wondering about who might have made another payoff, like I did. Seems to me you'd want to find the man who decided he *wasn't* going to make a payoff."

Chapter 12————————

I didn't bother phoning ahead this time to the widow Sommers. I figured things were getting down to the rough-edged state where a person could let the formalities slip on past like a leaf in the storm gutter. I had to ring the bell a couple of times and cool my heels before the front porch light went on. She had one of those glass-bead peek-a-boos in the door that lets a person inside look out at who's standing on the doorstep, and there was enough time that went by between when the light went on and she said anything, for me to know she'd taken the trouble to see who was calling. Despite that, she had to go through a little charade.

"Who is it?" she called through the door.

"The FBI. Open up or we'll break down the door."

A bolt was shot back and she opened the door, just enough to stick her head around its edge. "Why, Peter, I didn't expect to see you again tonight."

"I've learned a couple of things. We should talk some more."

"Oh? All right." She opened the door far enough for me to step through. As I went in I shot her a glance. At least I meant it to be a glance, but it lingered for a minute. She was holding a large white beach towel in front of her, and from the way she held it, I had the impression she didn't have on any clothes. She used one hip to nudge shut the door and gave me a little smile. "I was in the hot tub out back. Why don't you join me?"

"No thanks. I don't intend to be here that long."

She patted herself here and there with the towel. "Well then, maybe I'd better put on a robe."

She went past me down the hall toward one of the bedrooms, still clutching the towel across the front of her. She didn't bother wrapping any of it around her backside, and I'd been right. She didn't have on any clothes. And from the foxy little way she moved down the hallway, I knew she knew I'd be watching her. And after that I decided I'd better be watching myself. Maybe I'd have been smarter to bring Allison with me.

Sam the cat stuck her head around the kitchen doorway and bawled at me.

Jo came back wearing a belted, white terry-cloth robe. White worked well for her, contrasting starkly with her glossy black hair and the bright red lipstick she wore.

"Why don't we go out onto the patio?" she asked. "It's pleasant out there this evening. And my drink is there. Can I fix you one?"

"No thanks." I followed her out back. Amber lights spotted beneath the eaves of the house bathed the area in a warm glow. From the looks of the glass on the metal table at one side of the patio, she still was drinking gin and tonic. A little portable radio beside the glass was playing country western. She turned it down and sat with her drink in an aluminum tube chair with white plastic thongs stretched across the frame. I sat in a similar chair across from her.

"Have you learned something important?" she asked me.

"Yeah, I think I have."

"What's that?"

"Somebody got their hands on your husband's tapes and has been extorting money from half the retired military community around here."

She blinked at me but didn't say anything.

"At least I'm sure of the extortion part," I continued, "and I'm pretty sure your husband's tapes were involved. It would be too big a coincidence if they weren't. Nikki Scarborough was a part of it. I don't know if she was in up to her neck or was just being used by somebody else. Gus Wakefield was one of the intended victims, only somebody screwed up, mistaking him for his brother. That pretty well means your husband himself wasn't behind it. He wouldn't make that kind of mistake. I talked to another man this evening who was one of the extortion victims, and he told me about a third victim. All of these people were one-time patients of your husband. While Nikki Scarborough might have been a part of all this, I don't think she was smart enough to put it together and run the show. So that means somebody else."

"Do you have any idea who?"

"You, maybe."

She showed genuine surprise. "You're kidding."

"No, I'm not, Jo. I figure you're either behind it, or play a major role in it."

"That's just not true!"

We stared at each other for the better part of a minute. I didn't know if she was telling the truth or not. I would have had a better chance of gauging that in a complete stranger. I'd known Jo, not well maybe, but at least for enough years to tip askew whatever mechanism that might let me judge whether or not she was lying to me.

"Well," she said finally, "you don't believe me. That almost calls for another drink."

She started to get up, but I raised a hand and pushed air across the table. She sat back down. "You don't need another drink. And it doesn't really matter whether I believe you or not. If you aren't a big-league player in all this, you can still help me by telling me more than you have. Either about your husband's tapes, or the relationship he had with Nikki Scarborough, or some of those phone calls your husband had. Something. There is no way somebody outside of the family could have had access to the information on the tapes without a woman as bright as yourself having a suspicion or two about it."

"You're just guessing, Peter." Color was rising in her cheeks and her voice had a brittle edge. I'd finally scratched her under that cool, flirting-widow composure. I hadn't seen her like this before, not even when she'd broken down and cried for me in county jail.

"I have a dead husband and a dead girl friend," she told me. "To get the money to hire you to find out who killed my husband, I went to my family, which is the last thing I ever wanted to do. We are not a close-knit family, Peter. My brother and my mother think of me as very..."

She couldn't bring herself to say whatever came first to her mind. The word she finally settled for was "common."

"I had to do a little groveling for that money, and I'm certainly not about to grovel in front of the man I'm giving it to. And let's get something else settled. I didn't hire you to get to the bottom of any so-called extortion. I frankly don't care about any of that. All I want from you is for you to find out who killed my husband so the insurance company can't stiff me. If you're not good enough to do that, I'll find somebody who is."

Her hand rattled the ice in her glass, and she got to her feet. "And something else. Neither you nor anybody else is in any position, while in my home, to tell me whether or not I need another drink. You can sit there and decide whether you can handle all this while I'm getting it."

When she went past me, a large part of one long leg scissored out of the terry-cloth robe, but it wasn't because she wanted to show me a good time. And I didn't know what to do about it all. I still didn't think she was being honest with me. But she was angry.

I took a deep breath and stared up at the stars. There were two kinds of people I'd never learned how to deal with. One was drunk women. The other was angry women. I had a feeling that before much longer, Jo Sommers was going to be both of those. Which meant it was time for me to get out of there, but she wanted an answer from me. Did I want the job? Or, as she put it, was I good enough for it? With the restrictions she wanted to put on things, I wasn't ready to answer either one of them.

And then I heard something that didn't belong there right then. I heard the little squeak of warped wood I'd noticed the gate alongside the house made when anybody went through it. It was almost ten o'clock at night. Too late for the garbage man, and close friends would ring the doorbell.

The disc jockey on the country western station was talking to a phone-in listener. I turned up the volume, got up and crossed to the sliding glass door just as Jo was coming back out with her drink. I put a finger to my lips and motioned her back inside. She took me seriously, because I had the .38-caliber reminder of the war I'd been in out of its holster and in my hand. I'd decided to start carrying it around with me after finding the girl's body that afternoon. I stepped inside the house, and right then Sam the cat got the idea she wanted to go outside. I made a grab for her and missed, then just slid shut the door and locked it. Couldn't worry about the cat right then.

"We have company sneaking around the side of the house," I told Jo quietly. "Go to your husband's den or somewhere out of the way until you hear from me again. I'm going out the front door to come up behind them."

She went like the best little soldier in the world to the dead doctor's den. I trotted down the carpeted hallway, looked quickly through the spy port and eased open the door. Down the stairs and to the right. The visitor had left open the gate, which saved me from having to vault it in order to avoid the warpy squeak that had warned me of all this. I was through the gate and saw a shadowy movement at the back of the house. Somebody had just turned the corner ahead of me. I was still a couple of steps from going around the corner after him when it sounded like somebody tried to blow off the roof. There was an ear-cracking bang that had me rolling on the ground from instinct. When I came up into a squat, Sam the cat, hair standing straight, was going over the neighbor's fence. I peeked around the corner of the house. A figure was moving toward the other corner of the yard, holding an automatic pistol in an arm-extended, two-hand grip, looking for a gap in the bougainvillea to see into the patio and hot tub area. He was wearing a camouflage outfit like the one Allison had seen on the person going over the ridge at Big Sur. This one also had his face blackened, as if he were going to war. I intended to make him feel exactly that way, but he was a man finely experienced in these things. He sensed me and turned his entire body in my direction, then squeezed off two rounds that nicked the wooden shiplap in front of my face. I got off a quick shot of my own as I pulled back around the corner, rose up and then ran out at an angle to my left, which I figured would be the place he'd least expect to see me appear, but he already was gone.

The blast must have come from something he lobbed over the latice walls into the patio. There still were wisps of thin smoke in the air and the smell of explosive. This registered as I reversed myself and ran back down the side of the house with the gate. I wasn't going to go around the corner the way the mad bomber had. He'd be expecting that. I thought that with luck I could go around the front of the house and find him slipping around in the ice plant alongside the garage. But as it turned out, that was too much to hope for. He already was out in the street and running hard by the time I got around to the front. There was no sense in sending a bullet after him just to let him know I was on his ass. I jammed the .38 back into the holster, tossed my sports jacket on the front stairs and took off down the street after him.

He rounded the nearby corner and headed west, toward the ocean. I was thirty to forty yards behind him. As I rounded the corner after him, he turned his head slightly, not to get a look at me, just to listen to the sound of my clobbering shoes behind him.

I figured I had about ten seconds to make up my mind what I was going to do. I stay fit, but if he was a dedicated runner, he'd leave me dogged out in short order. He was running as hard as he'd been when I first saw him out in the street. He wasn't pulling out ahead of me, but I wasn't gaining on him, either. I was trying to do this weighty thinking, cool as a cucumber, when an old fellow wearing a tam-o'-shanter and argyle sweater came around a far corner walking his short-legged dachshund. They threw my man off his stride.

The dog yipped at the running figure and jerked his leash out of the old man's hand. The running figure took a startled veer, swinging his arms up and pointing the pistol in the direction of the man and his dog, appraised the situation, lowered the pistol and resumed running. I had gained twenty yards on him. I vaulted the dog and shot a grin at the wide-eyed old chap at the curb. I pulled the .38 back out of its holster just as the jungle fighter ahead of me realized he'd come to the end of a cul-de-sac. That brought me five yards closer. I was bringing up the .38 when he dashed down along the side of a house overlooking the shoreline and scrambled over a back fence. I put the .38 back in its holster and went over the same fence off to the right of where he'd gone over.

It turned out I'd been as good as he was at running, but I wasn't as good at going over fences. By the time I got over it, the man I was chasing had scrambled down a long sandy bank and was slogging up the beach to the north. I knew I'd never catch him. So I did the next best thing. I took out the .38 again and sat down with my back braced against the fence, and with deliberate care gave him something to think about by emptying the revolver after him. It would have been uncommon luck to have hit him, and I figured he was experienced enough to know that, but by the last couple of rounds I sent after him, he was jittering around some at the bang the .38 made. At least I'd made a point. He'd know somebody else was lugging around a handgun. He wouldn't be all cool and cocksure the next time we met.

There'd been enough of a ruckus to make somebody call the sheriff's office. A couple of deputies had arrived by the time I got back to the house. Their cars were parked with winking roof lights at the curb. Jo had told them what had happened up to the point I'd last gone out of her life, and I brought them up-to-date on the chase down the street, mentioning the man and the dachshund if they wanted confirmation. After I'd spoken my piece, one of the deputies went out to his vehicle to radio another unit to get somebody searching that stretch of beach where I'd last seen the man in the cammies. I doubted that anything would come from that. Deputy sheriffs are only human. There had been a killer some while back, terrorizing my mountain up home, Mount Tamalpais in Marin County. It was a 2,500-foot-high, double-domed rise of ground offering two hundred miles of surrounding hiking trails and getting-away-from-it-allness, just nine miles away from downtown San Francisco. Three women had been slain while hiking or walking the trails of Mount Tam over a twenty-one-month period. The bodies of three other women and a male companion of one of them had been found at the nearby Point Reyes National Seashore. A suspect finally was caught and was awaiting trial for killing another woman down in Santa Cruz County. But before his capture, Mount Tamalpais had become voluntarily off-limits to the hundreds of Bay Area residents who had regularly enjoyed its restorative presence, and in the Sand Dollar Bar and Restaurant in Stinson Beach, at the mountain's oceanside foot, I'd heard a Marin County deputy sheriff admit to a cocktail waitress that he no longer took rest breaks, as had been his habit during lonely night patrols, in a clearing off a secluded road on the mountain. He was afraid somebody would come out of the dark and shoot him. That was a lawman talking. And what would be true for a lawman in Marin County would be true for a lawman in Monterey County. Two-man patrol units would be one thing. Having a buddy to cover you was a comfortable feeling. But few men would go alone into the night looking for a man wearing cammies with blackened face, carrying a pistol and who knows what else, including hand grenades maybe. Because that was what the other deputy had determined was lobbed over the back patio hedge, making the big noise. And if I hadn't heard the gate squeak—God bless warped wood—Jo and I probably would be on our way to the county morgue. The glass patio doors were pitted and cracked and there were shreds and bits of metal all across the patio and on the table and seats where we'd sat. The radio was on the ground nearby, gutted and burned.

The deputies knew about the murder of Jo's husband on Friday, but they didn't know of the connection between Jo and the girl killed that afternoon down at Big Sur. If Wally Hamlin were in town, I would have told them about the girl, and they probably would have gotten in touch with him at home and pursued the matter further that evening. But since Wally wasn't in town, I didn't want anybody else around just then. I wanted cops out of it for a while. This was one of those times when only I might be the fellow to learn what was there to be learned. And I wasn't too sure how far I might get.

So the deputies finished taking down information and left, telling Jo a detective probably would be by to interrogate her further the next day. That was the word they used, *interrogate*. It's part of the academy training. The way they're taught to make out reports. The reports don't acknowledge they deal with men and women with passion in their blood or despondency in their bones. The reports refer to Male Number One or Female Number Two and use words like *interrogate*. I didn't bother to tell them that I was going to do my best to see that Jo Sommers wasn't around there the next day for interrogation by detectives, by men with blackened faces or by anybody else. Any interrogating that was going to be done was going to be done that night. By me.

Chapter 13 ————

I was the one to see the deputies to the front door and out of the house. I hadn't noticed when Jo fell by the wayside and disappeared. On the way back through the house I glanced into the front room and checked the bedroom and sewing room, peered into her late husband's den and walked through the kitchen.

Out in the patio, her terry-cloth robe was thrown over a chair at the table, and Jo was back in the hot tub.

"You're a pretty cool cookie," I told her, "coming back out here after what just happened."

"You don't think he'll come back, do you, whoever it was?"

"No, I don't, as a matter of fact. Not just yet."

"Then why don't you take off your clothes and join me? It's very soothing, after what we've just been through."

"No thanks. We have to talk some more, you know. Especially after what we've just been through."

"I suppose we do. Why don't you go and get me a drink first. Gin and tonic, if you please. Everything's in the kitchen. You could probably do with one yourself."

"You're probably right. If the man in the cammies comes back in the meantime, tell him to lighten up. I'll bring a drink for him, too."

"And I'll invite him to join me in the tub. There's no reason we can't all be civilized about things."

She was smiling when I turned and went back through the pitted, sliding glass door and into the kitchen. I didn't worry about the family budget when I poured the drinks. The amount of gin I'd seen Jo throw back since that afternoon didn't seem to have had any discernible effect, and I was due for a little kicking back myself. Maybe if we both got drunk, she'd tell me things she hadn't told me before. The more I thought about it, the better I liked the idea. I found larger glasses. She had some of those French barrel glasses meant for canning. I poured the drinks I'd already made into two of them and added more gin. Then I constructed a couple of more of the same in two more of the barrel glasses, found a metal tray on top of the refrigerator, loaded it with the drinks and strolled back out to the patio. Hell, this job could turn out to be fun even, if I could just forget about Allison.

When I put the tray down on the shrapnel-littered tabletop, Jo murmured approvingly. "There always was a certain panache about you I approved of, Peter," she told me.

I walked over to the tub platform and lifted one of the glasses to her waiting hand. "Yeah, well, once in a while I get tired of projecting such a stern figure."

"I could make a naughty little wordplay with that."

"Please don't. We still have things to discuss. I just decided, what the hell, we might as well do it in a lighter mood."

"I'm glad you decided that. Cheers."

I lifted my own glass in toast and we drank. It tasted uncommonly good.

"Come join me," Jo said.

"In the tub? I already said no to that."

"I know you did. But you're a grown man. You can change your mind about things. I can't have you asking me all sorts of questions with you all clothed and solemn-faced, despite the drink in your hand, while I'm here all vulnerable and naked in my hot tub. It would give you too much of a psychological advantage. Humor me, please, kind sir."

Sometimes there's a randy side to me that slips out and makes hay of the steady-as-you-go image I try to project. I sat at the table and took off my shoes, then stood and began peeling off my duds. In for a penny, in for a pound. When I stepped out of my shorts, as gracefully as any man can, which isn't very, Jo Sommers whistled. I didn't let it bother me. I was sure I wasn't among the first half dozen men she'd seen without their underwear on. I climbed up to the platform with the tray carrying the other two drinks and put it on a shelf built onto the outer rim of the tub. Then I climbed down a ladder on the inside wall of the tub into the warm, warm water, lifted my own drink off the tray and sat on the underwater bench opposite Jo. I lifted the glass again in a little salute and drank. She held her own outsized glass just below her mouth, staring at me over it.

"I like this side of you," she said quietly, "the way you drop your—inhibitions."

"Yeah, well, don't get too comfy about it all. I still have to ask you some things you're not going to want to talk about."

"But at least we'll be equal in the eyes of God, while you're asking them."

"And the eyes of anybody else who might wander through."

"You're not expecting anybody, are you? Lady Allison, perhaps?"

"No, I'm not expecting anybody."

"Good. Neither am I." She took another drink of

the gin and tonic, then made a rather elaborate arc of her arm, which raised one breast out of the water, as she placed the glass on the outer shelf near where she was sitting. She settled back down into the water and crossed her arms in front of herself. "Well, Daddy, I'm waiting. Do whatever bad to me you're going to do."

I brought my mind back to business. "How long were you and your husband married?"

The question surprised her. She blinked at me a time or two before replying. "It's been years. Six, seven maybe."

"Where did you meet?"

"At a swimming-pool party up in Sacramento. Woody still was practicing then. He was seeing somebody at an air force base near there."

"Mather?"

"No, that wasn't it."

"McClellan?"

"That's the one. I'd been visiting a friend I'd gone to school with when we both lived up in Washington. She'd been invited to the party and took me along. Woody knew somebody else who knew the people having the party. We were both in swimsuits when we were introduced. We were attracted to each other instantly. We made love for the first time that evening, back at his motel. At the time he was living in San Mateo. I still lived in San Francisco. We saw each other frequently, after that. We married within a month."

"When did you move down here?"

"Three or four months after we were married. It took us that long to find a place acceptable to both of us. Here."

"Why did you move down here?"

"Why not? It's beautiful, when the sun's out. The temperature is mild. And in Woody's case, of course, there were so many people he knew living in the area."

"Ex-patients?"

"Not necessarily. Some, of course, but other people as well."

She reached back to fetch her gin and tonic again but didn't exaggerate the effort this time to give me another flash of her body.

"Did he continue to practice down here?"

"No, that's when he gave it up."

"Tired of other people's problems?"

"Not necessarily. He continued to lecture, at schools here on the Coast and back East. And he wanted time to think, and he wanted to write."

"Write what?"

She shrugged her thin shoulders. "Professional things."

"Was he working on something now?"

"Yes. His first book-length manuscript."

"Can I look at it?"

"Of course. But I doubt if you'd much understand it. I tried reading it once. They have their own language, you know."

"I'd still like to see it."

"All right."

"And I'd like you to show me where he kept the tapes of his patient visits."

She held the French glass in front of her chin and stared into the tub water. "You really think that's it, then?"

"What's it?"

"That somebody was using his tapes to—get money from people." She looked up at me. "That that's the reason somebody killed Woody and Nikki."

"Yes, I do. But since your husband was killed, somebody's figured out that your husband wasn't the one behind it. Probably because the extortion

has continued after he was killed. They found out
Nikki was a part of it. That's why she's dead. And
now they've decided that you're the one behind it.
That's why somebody lobbed that grenade in here
tonight. And it won't stop at that. It didn't work this
time, but they'll come after you again. So it isn't just
whether or not you'll get your husband's insurance
money that's important now. In fact, that grenade
tonight will weigh in your favor, so far as the
insurance people are concerned. But what you and
I have to see to now, Jo, is that you're alive to collect
it."

We sat quietly. I left her alone to let her think
things through. She'd been having a lot of distrac-
tions recently, but she was bright enough to see
where things stood if she was left to herself for a
bit.

By the time she'd finished her drink and was
nibbling on a piece of ice, she seemed to have made
up her mind. She made a little nod of her head, then
took a mighty breath and stood up in the tub. The
water came to a couple of inches below her belly
button. She crossed over to my side and leaned past
me to put the glass on the tray and get one of the
fresh drinks. Then she passed one hand through her
hair and settled herself sideways on my lap and
looped one arm around my neck.

"You're not going to like what I have to tell you,"
she said quietly.

"What I like doesn't matter. Finding a killer and
saving your life do."

"That's what I've decided."

"Were you and . . ."

She turned her head and gave me a quick kiss on
the mouth to shut me up. "No, let me think a
moment more. I'll tell you in my own way."

She sipped her drink and rested her head alongside my own, gazing off into the distance again. She wasn't really trying to tease me, the way she had been earlier. She was just trying to establish a little intimacy to make it easier for her to tell me her role in a sustained effort to screw money out of the local citizens. But that didn't make it any easier for me to try to maintain the aloofness such a moment should require of a serious investigator. Not when he was sitting down without his clothes on in a tub of hot water and a very pretty and naked young woman was sitting on his lap. I tried to keep things under control as best I could, without total success. It didn't matter, really. Anything my own body was doing didn't seem to bother her any. Maybe it was a little test she subjected her gentlemen friends to in the hot tub. She could separate the dead from the living that way. I was among the living.

"It wasn't really my idea," she began finally. She took another sip of the gin and tonic, then laid her head back next to mine again, talking across the tub into the night air. "It started as a lark, at first. At least that's the way I was approached about it. A friend suggested it one day when we were talking. I had been complaining about what a tightwad Woody was. I'd asked Woody not long before if he couldn't spare a little more money for the household budget. I picked a bad moment, apparently. He refused, in a—rude and vulgar way. I told my friend about it. My friend said, well, why don't you get the money from Woody in another way? And we talked about the tapes. And how they could be used in such a way to cause apoplexy among some of these old fogies Woody knew from his past. My friend was very clever and inventive. We had drinks and talked about it some more, and finally I figured, oh, what the hell, why not?"

"Extortion? And you said, oh, what the hell, why not?"

She put one hand across my lips. "It was pillow talk, darling. Woody was halfway across the country just then giving one of his lectures. My friend and I were giving each other a great deal of pleasure that afternoon. Anything at all seemed all right, under the circumstances. So I brought out some of the tapes and we listened to them together. You'd be appalled at some of the ghastly things these people have done."

"Or had happen to them."

"Yes, that too." She drank some more. "Anyway, that's how it all started. Almost offhandedly. During an afternoon of pillow talk."

I shifted my position. "Go sit back down across the way."

"Why, darling? Don't you like a girl to sit on your lap?"

"I love a girl to sit on my lap. Too much so, as you're well aware unless you've given yourself a shot of Novocain in the butt. You've got to let me concentrate on things for a few minutes, or you're apt to end up like Nikki and your husband."

She gave me a pout, but got to her feet and waded back to the other side of the tub. She had a marvelous-looking bottom, that girl.

She settled herself across from me, tucked her feet up on the bench and rested the glass on her knees.

"How did you know which tapes to listen to?"

"Woody had a list, keying the codes he used on the cassettes with the names of his patients. He showed it to me once. In case anything happened to him, he wanted certain of the tapes sent to a school back East. He thought they could be important to others in the field."

"So you could pull out the tapes keyed to names you recognized."

"That's right."

"Are you going to tell me the name of your friend?"

"I'm not sure yet. I've never been one to kiss and tell, darling. It might not be necessary for you to know. It's the killer's name you want."

I let that one go for the minute. Like a lot of us, she had a stupid side to her. "What did you do after you listened to the tapes?"

"We made copies of the ones he would be using. I don't really know a great deal more of how he went about it than that. I wasn't an active part of the actual contact with people, or getting the money or anything like that. Nikki was, in a way, as you've already guessed. I know that during the past weekend she was given some money by somebody. It was to be set up so she appeared to be an innocent party to what really was going on. She told me that the night we met."

"Friday."

"That's right. She said somebody was going to leave her an envelope with the money in it at her stall at the fairgrounds. Maybe she was involved even more than that, though, if she had copies of the tapes themselves."

"And she still had the money as well. Level with me, Jo. You know she was more involved than just being a money drop. Why would she have had copies of the tapes?"

She squirmed around a little and put her glass back on the shelf. "She made some phone calls, to the people they were asking money from. She wouldn't speak to them herself. When she got the right party on the line she would play a portion of the tape over the phone, then hang up. A day or so later, my friend would either telephone the person on the tape or write to him and suggest that a certain sum of money be left at a given place at a particular time."

"Wonderful," I told her. "The mail thing makes it a federal offense as well."

"It doesn't matter. You're not going to turn me in, are you? I really had so little to do with it, after all, except for that one day when we talked about it and my friend copied the tapes that he did. He and Nikki were the real operators. I've hardly even seen any of the money they've got. Even though it all started when I complained about how tight Woody was, I didn't really do it for that so much as I did it as a joke. For the consternation it would cause these old curmudgeons."

"Your husband and Nikki dead? That kind of consternation?"

"No, of course not," she said, looking away. "I didn't know it would really go anywhere. I mean, I didn't know people would actually pay money to keep some of these problems from the past a secret. I wouldn't, I know. And I have had a few problems of my own, believe me. I didn't hear anything on any of the tapes I listened to that seemed that devastating."

"How much money have you gotten from it?"

"A few hundred dollars, is all. I was supposed to get some of that money Nikki was given Friday night. Then, I was to get quite a bit more sometime soon. At least that's what my friend said."

I shook my head and stared at the stars. "Have you talked to this clever, inventive friend of yours since your husband was killed?"

"Yes, we spoke earlier today."

"Did it ever come up in the conversation that it might be a good idea to just break off the extortion efforts?"

"No. Neither one of us thought it had anything to do with Woody's death. And we didn't know about Nikki. We talked about other things, mostly." She reached back and finished the drink on the shelf. "Are you going to have that other gin and tonic?"

"No, I'm not."

"May I have it then, please?"

I put my own glass on the tray and carried the fresh drink across to Jo. She took the glass, then put one hand behind my knee to keep me there a moment, and looked up at me with the first signs of doubt on her face.

"Do you think I'm a bad woman?"

"Who knows what that is? No, I don't think you're necessarily a bad woman. I think in this one instance you've been awfully stupid. And frankly, I don't think your boyfriend is all that clever, either."

"Too bad," she said quietly. "I wanted you to tell me I was a bad woman. Then I wanted you to take me inside and make love. It's about time, don't you think?"

"Oh, Jo..." I turned away and climbed up out of the tub. She'd put a couple of towels on a lower step of the platform stairs. I took one of them and dried myself, then climbed back into my clothes.

"I think you'd better tell me who your friend is," I told her.

"Is it really absolutely necessary?"

"Yes, it is. You don't know enough about what's been going on, if you've been telling me the truth."

"I have been."

"Okay. So here's where things stand. Somebody's after you, and they might be after him as well. He probably doesn't know about Nikki yet, and he doesn't know about the grenade attack here, unless he's a cop."

She laughed. "He's not a cop."

"So you'd better tell me and let me go talk to him. The killer might have gotten his name from Nikki before he shot her. Or something else down there might have pointed in his direction. And if I can get your boyfriend to level with me, maybe he can tell me something that'll give me an idea who the killer is."

"I suppose you're right." She had a drink of fresh gin and tonic. I didn't know how she did it. Maybe she had a metabolic system that squeezed the liquor out of her pores into the hot water as fast as she drank it.

"Alex Kilduff," she said finally.

"The bartender?"

"That's right. He's a lovely young man, in many ways."

"Sure. A real sweetheart, probably. I should have thought of him myself."

"You've been busy, darling."

"Right. Do you know where I could find him now?"

"No. At that bar where he works, perhaps."

"Okay, I'll go looking for him." I picked up the other towel and held it up to her. "Now, how about getting out of there and putting some things in a suitcase."

"Whatever for?"

"I want you to go check into a motel somewhere. Not around here, either. Maybe over near Salinas."

"You think the man who bombed us will be back?"

"It's a possibility. I'll follow you out of town a ways to make sure nobody's tailing you, then I'll go find Alex. And I'd like you to give me another key to the place. The cops took the one from under the tub."

"Why do you want a key?"

"After I've talked to Alex, I'm coming back here to spend the night."

"Then you do think the killer will be back."

"The only question is when."

Chapter 14 ————————

While Jo was getting her stuff together, I phoned Allison at the motel. I told her I'd be by later to pick up my shaving gear and a couple of other things, but that I wouldn't be spending the night there.

"Aha," she said in that quiet way of hers.

"It's not exactly what you think. There was an attempt on Jo's life earlier."

"What happened?"

"Somebody lobbed a grenade into the patio. Luckily, nobody was out there at the time. But whoever did it might come back. I'm sending Jo out of town for the night."

"And what will you be doing?"

"I have to find somebody and ask them a few questions. Then I'm coming back to Jo's place and sit up with the mice to see if the grenade man comes back."

"And what if he does come back?"

"I'll capture the devil, what do you suppose?"

She told me to watch my moves around Jo Sommers. I told her I'd be doing my best.

I went back outside and looked around for the cat. She didn't seem to be in the neighborhood. I didn't blame her. Jo changed the cat's water and left out some dry food for it. She said there was a flapped hatch in the side of the garage Sam used, and she'd probably come on back home when her ears quit ringing.

Jo backed out the family Mercedes, and I carried down the suitcase she'd packed. I went back through the house and left a couple of lights on low in the front room and the late doctor's study. Jo told me she'd phone me later to let me know the name and phone number of the motel where she'd be staying. I drove behind her back out to the highway and up over the Carmel hill. She took the Salinas turnoff. I stayed with her for about three miles, gradually dropping back. When I was satisfied nobody else was following her, I turned back and drove on over to downtown Carmel. It was after ten o'clock, but I still wasn't hungry. Hand grenades can do that to a person. I went looking for Alex.

At the Duck's Quack they told me he'd gone off duty about an hour earlier. He'd had a drink and then left. The bartender now on duty gave me the names of a couple of other bars where I might look for him. I went to the places and looked, but Alex hadn't been to either one of them that night, so I went back to the Duck's Quack and tried to wheedle out an address or telephone number for young Alex Kilduff. I'd ordered a drink this time, a weak bourbon and water, and paid with a ten-dollar bill. The bartender, a tall brisk man approaching thirty with a thick, dark mustache, put my change on the bar and told me it was against house policy to give out information to do with the help. I didn't know if the timing was a coincidence or not. I slid the five-dollar bill into the bar gutter and asked if he'd try calling Alex at home himself and tell Alex I needed to talk to him.

"It's important," I told him. "Tell him we met at Gus Wakefield's party Saturday night. Tell him I was the spy with the stunning blonde. My name's Pete.

He might not remember me, but he'll remember the blonde. Her name was Allison."

The bartender nodded. When he'd finished making a drink order for a cocktail waitress, he went to a phone behind the bar and dialed a number. Somebody answered on the other end and they talked for a moment, then the bartender turned my way with a little nod and pointed toward an extension phone on the wall by the cocktail waitress station. I lifted the receiver and we exchanged greetings.

"What's up?" he asked.

"We need to talk. It's important. Only I'd like it to be someplace a little more private than the bar here. Maybe we could meet somewhere."

"What do we need to talk about?"

"Jo Sommers and Nikki Scarborough. I think the murder of Jo's husband has something to do with it, too." I tried to keep my voice low, but the waitress was hovering nearby and gave me a quick glance. She was trying to listen in.

"What do those people mean to you?" Alex asked.

"Look, it really is impossible to tell you more about it right here. You know what your own bar is like. Can't we meet somewhere? It's to your own advantage."

He thought it over some. "I think I'd rather keep this to just a phone conversation," he told me. "I'll tell you what. Do you know where the Barnyard shopping center is?"

I stiffened. "Yes, I know where it is."

"There's a pay telephone there next to the supermarket. I happen to know the number of the phone. You can go on down there. I'll phone the number in twenty minutes. If it's busy, I'll keep trying until I get you. But I doubt if there'll be anybody around at this time of night."

"Okay. I'll drive on down and wait for your call."

I went back out to my car. The night was having its ups and downs. I would rather have seen Alex in person, for a number of reasons. But at least the pay phone he was sending me to sounded like the one Larry Pitt told me he'd been sent to before he was told to take his envelope full of money to the Hog's Breath.

I got there a few minutes early and the phone was free. I checked the phone book there to make sure Alex didn't have a listing, for his phone number, if not his address. He didn't. That seemed a bit odd, for a bartender with an obviously active social life. The telephone rang exactly when Alex had told me he'd be phoning, and it was him.

"Now, I don't have a great deal of time—Pete, was it?"

"That's right, Peter Bragg. But you'll want to take the time to hear me out. Some things happened today you might not know about, and your name came up in the course of things in such a way as to make me think you might be in a bit of physical danger."

"Who exactly are you, Mr. Bragg?"

"I'm a private investigator from San Francisco who's known Jo Sommers for a number of years. When I learned her husband had been murdered, and that she was a suspect, I got in touch with her and offered to do some digging into things for her."

"That was generous of you, I'm sure. But I hardly know those people. Dr. and Mrs. Sommers, and who else did you say?"

"Nikki Scarborough."

"That name doesn't ring any bells at all."

"That's odd. Jo Sommers told me you knew her. And I saw you in what looked like a pretty serious conversation with her Sunday night at the Duck's Quack. She has a pottery studio down at Big Sur."

"Oh, yes. I remember now."

"Thought you might. At least she used to have a pottery studio at Big Sur."

"She moved?"

"She died."

He might be clever and inventive, as Jo had said, but he wasn't able to mask the quick intake of breath. "I hope that you're joking, Mr. Bragg."

"It's no joke. She was shot through the head while trying to run away from somebody who was after her. It happened while I was driving out to see her. Something had frightened her earlier and she wanted to talk to me. She also left me a couple of audio tapes that turned out to be copies of tapes that belonged to Dr. Sommers. Then this evening, I was over at the Sommers home when——"

But he didn't want to hear any more. The bloody young fool hung up on me. I mouthed an off-color word or two and hung up the phone. I stood there for another five minutes, hoping he'd think better of it and call me back. He didn't. I dialed the Duck's Quack again, but then hung up before the call went through. I'd do better getting back to the Sommers home, in case he tried calling Jo.

I drove back to my motel first. It only took about eight minutes.

"What's wrong?" Allison asked when I breezed in and headed for the bathroom to pack a toilet kit.

"Things are starting to happen," I told her. "It turns out some people got their hands on tape recordings made by the late Dr. Sommers, in sessions with his patients. Some of the former patients live around here now, and the people with the tapes were using them to extort money from the ex-patients. I think that's why the doctor was killed, and also that girl today. And according to Jo Sommers, the brains behind it all was Mr. Personality behind the bar at Gus Wakefield's party, Alex Kilduff."

"But he's just a boy."

"He's old enough. To sleep around with other men's wives, and to go off to war and kill people, if need be, like a lot of other kids have done. I just tried to warn him by phone that some war might be coming his way, but he hung up on me."

I zippered shut the kit, gave Allison a quick kiss and headed for the door. "Can't talk more, right now. I'm going back to the Sommers home and try to get in touch with him again. If anybody else should call here, don't tell them where I'm at. I'll phone you later."

"Okay, boss," she told me on my way out.

Ten minutes later I was parked up the street from the Sommers home. I sat a few minutes observing the house and the street. Nothing seemed out of the ordinary. I got out of the car and closed the door quietly, then went around and opened the trunk. I got out the other traveling case, the one with the .45 automatic pistol inside. The .38 revolver I'd been carrying since Big Sur was a fairly companionable little weapon, but if the hand grenade man came in my direction again, I wanted the .45. More bang for the buck.

I moved briskly on down the street, went up the front stairs of the Sommers place two at a time and let myself inside. I squeezed shut the door and stood quietly listening. I didn't hear or sense any other presence, but I took out the .45 and went through the house quickly. It was empty. I went into the doctor's den and used the phone there to dial the Duck's Quack again. A cocktail waitress answered. I asked for the bartender.

"I'm the guy who wanted to talk to Alex a little earlier," I told him. "I need another little favor. I'll stop by tomorrow and leave an envelope with a little something more in it for you. What's your name?"

"Johnny, but that's not necessary. What's the favor?"

"I'd like you to call Alex again and give him a brief message. We were talking earlier, but got disconnected."

"Okay. What's the message?"

"Tell him somebody tried to kill Jo Sommers tonight." Johnny whistled in my ear. "Is this serious?"

"Indeed it is."

"Okay, pal. Let me write that name down. Jo who?"

"Sommers." I spelled it for him. "Can you do that right away? It's important that he get the message."

"I'll see to it," he told me.

We hung up. I took off my sports jacket and folded it over a chair, then sat down and waited for Alex Kilduff to phone. I just hoped that this time I'd be able to keep him on the line.

After ten minutes it began to look as if keeping him on the line wasn't going to be a problem. I went out into the kitchen and stuck my nose into the refrigerator. There was a lot of diet cola but no leftovers. I went back into the den and fixed myself another bourbon and water. Maybe instead of phoning, young Alex would come on out to visit with the widow Sommers. Or maybe he was just going to fold up his tent and leave town. It would be the smart thing to do.

I crossed to the fireplace mantel and stood looking at the little models there. Machine gun, plane, ship, ambulance and what might have been a prison camp diorama. They made me think of old wars.

A few minutes later I shook myself out of the past and realized my drink was empty. I put the glass back over by the wet bar and went across the room to the doctor's rolltop desk. It wasn't locked. In fact it didn't have any locks on it. I went through it but didn't find anything that needed locking away anyhow. Two of the drawers were empty. The others held bills and receipts and material to do with his lecturing here and there. I realized then I'd forgotton all about getting the book manuscript from Jo before I sent her into the night. Since it wasn't in his desk, there must have been somewhere else he kept his professional papers. I went scouting around. While on my way down the hall I went into Jo's bedroom to turn on a table lamp and switch on a small, color television set mounted from the ceiling in one corner. I tuned in a late movie and left the sound on low. The lady of the house was supposed to be tucking herself in for the night.

The doctor's bedroom was pretty utilitarian. The dresser drawers held shirts fresh from the laundry and handkerchiefs, stockings and underwear and sweaters. In the closet were shoes and slacks and jackets. A bedside stand had a box of tissues and a pair of earplugs. Until the grenade had gone off in the back patio, I wondered why anybody in that neighborhood would need a pair of earplugs. Maybe he didn't like the sound of foghorns.

Phones jangled around the house. I trotted back up to the doctor's den.

"Hello?"

I was greeted by what I took to be a startled silence. At least, nobody answered, and I had the feeling that a man's voice must have surprised whoever it was. I also had the feeling that I'd outclevered myself. I had that feeling when the line went dead. It could have been Alex. Or it could have been the man in the cammies. I dialed the Duck's Quack and Johnny the bartender answered. He was able to recognize my voice by now.

"Were you able to get the message to Alex?" I asked him.

"No, he didn't answer. But the message seemed important enough for me to send one of the guys at the bar over to his place to tell him in person. The guy just got back. He said Alex wasn't at home, and the place was dark. I'll keep trying to call him until closing time."

"I appreciate the effort, but would you mind telling me something else?"

"What's that?"

"Why is it house policy not to give out addresses and phone numbers of the bartenders? Cocktail waitresses, I could understand, but a bunch of bartenders?"

"Well, we had this married guy working here a while back. He used to play around a little. Other women he'd meet here. He didn't want any of them calling his home. You can understand."

"Yeah, I can understand, but Alex isn't married, is he?"

"No, but he doesn't like his address or phone number spread around. He's always been a little funny that way."

"How long have you known him?"

"A year, maybe a little longer. Ever since he came to work here."

"Has he worked anywhere else around town that you know of?"

"Don't think so. He got on here right after he came out from back East somewhere."

"When's he scheduled to work again?"

"He opens up tomorrow morning. Ten o'clock. If I don't reach him at home by the time I leave here, I'll leave a note for him with your message."

"Thanks. You've been a big help."

I was going through the rest of the house when Jo phoned. She gave me the phone number of the motel she was staying at on the outskirts of Salinas.

"Has anything else happened?" she asked.

"Nothing special. I bobbled a telephone conversation with Alex. He hung up on me before I could learn anything useful. Since then, he's quit answering his phone and his house is dark, according to people at the bar where he works. You wouldn't have his address and phone number, would you?"

"I can give you the phone number. I don't have his address, but I can tell you how to find it. I've been there once or twice."

She told me he lived in a quaint wooden home just off Lighthouse Avenue near the boundary line between Pacific Grove and Monterey. "It doesn't look like much," she told me. "But the rent's reasonable."

I wrote down the directions. "Something else," I told her. "You didn't give me the manuscript your husband had been working on."

"Oh, I forgot. There's an old chest in a back corner of the study. I moved his chair up against it. The manuscript's in there. Along with some of his tapes. At least all the ones Alex copied."

An idea I should have had earlier gave me a little jolt. "Just hold the phone a minute, will you? I want to take a look inside that chest."

I put down the receiver, went over to where she'd put the chair and pulled it away. The chest was an old one, made of dark wood and leather with metal straps and hinges. I lifted the lid. The insides were a jumble. The manuscript was in a box on top. Beneath that were cassettes and file folders and all sorts of papers and documents bound with rubber bands. There must have been thirty to forty little cassettes, all of them bearing a combination of numbers and letters. The doctor's code. I went back to the phone.

"Okay, I found the manuscript, but suddenly I'm more interested in the tapes. Do you know which ones Alex copied?"

"No. He used Woody's code list to pick and choose."

"Where's the code list?"

"I don't know. It used to be in his desk, but when I was looking for it earlier today I couldn't find it. He must have moved it."

"Why were you looking for it?"

"I told you. He wanted me to send some of his material back East, after he died. It's just one of the chores to be gotten out of the way. Why? What did you want with it?"

"It could lead me to the man who wants all of you people dead. He must be on one of the tapes. If I had the code list, I might be able to find him."

"I wish I could help you. But I wouldn't know where to look."

"I thought you told me earlier that your husband's tapes were stored in the garage."

"Most of them are. But those dealing with patients he had most recently, just before he retired, and ones involving people now living in the Monterey area, he kept in the study. So they'd be handy, if any of those people wanted to consult him again."

"That helps narrow it down. Maybe I'll listen to a few of them. I'll give you a call in the morning. Don't check out until you hear from me. You might have to stay there another day."

"Peter, do you really think that man will be going back there tonight?"

"That's what I'm here to find out. Why?"

"Why do you think? It's a perfect setup, darling, if Allison thinks you're spending the night at my place. You could really come spend it with me. It's only a thirty-minute drive from there. Think about it." And then she hung up.

I stared at the phone a minute, then got up and walked back to the rolltop desk. I was going to give it a little more thorough search than I had the time before, looking for something resembling the code sheet. Then my eye was caught by a small, framed photograph of Jo hanging on the wall over the desk. She was standing on the front walk outside, wearing a riding costume—gray jodhpurs, blue jacket and riding helmet. She was just putting on a glove, and staring into the camera with a little smile on her mouth, the same expression she showed you when she was about to say something of a suggestive nature to do with the bedroom...She was a lot more trouble than I needed right then, I decided. I put myself to work going through the desk.

Five minutes later the phone rang. It was Jo again. This time she was all business.

"Peter, you started me thinking about those tapes. You know, there was one of them that Alex seemed to feel was much more important than the others. He called it the 'Big Casino.' That was before he listened to it, even. As if the others were just a prelude to that particular one." She paused a moment. "I should have known then that there was something more to this than he first let on."

"How could he have known it was important even before he listened to it? Did he have your husband's code sheet at the time?"

"He had it, but he didn't use it to find that particular tape. He was searching through the chest for another tape he'd seen listed on the code sheet. But then he came across this other tape and told me it was the important one. He must have recognized something about Woody's code."

"That means your husband's code must have a practical foundation. It wasn't something he just made up."

"I suppose it must."

"Did you know who was on it?"

"No, he didn't even listen to it just then. He just took it with the others to make copies."

"Did you notice the code that was on it?"

"I saw it, but I don't remember it all. It had a letter or two, then a two-digit number. It was a number in the thirties."

"How do you remember that?"

"It has to do with age, darling. Women remember that sort of thing. Will that help?"

"It'll help."

"Will I get a kiss for it the next time I see you?"

"At least that."

She purred for a moment and hung up. I went back to the chest and took out the tape cassettes. I went through them quickly. Two of them had numbers in the thirties as part of their coding. I picked out another one as well. It was marked *.30 B M 1919A4.* Jo said the tape Alex felt was important was in the thirties but only had a couple of letters. This one had more than a couple, but it seemed to ring a bell in my own mind.

I put the first of the short thirty codes on the portable recorder but only listened to a bit of the first side of the tape. It was pretty tame stuff. The patient was a man with ulcers and insomnia. He'd spent a year in Vietnam. Nothing out of the ordinary there. Struck me it would be the normal condition for any man who had to spend a year out there. It wasn't hardly the stuff of blackmail and extortion.

The other was a different kettle of fish. Sommers was talking to a man under considerable stress. The odd thing about the tape was that it didn't begin the way Jo said they usually did. It just began with a man speaking in midsentence. It was pretty raw stuff. I had the impression it was the man's first session with the doctor.

"We didn't know where they were supposed to be . . . We

didn't know their mission. Didn't know they were without escort—" Something like a sob shook the man's voice. *"Jesus, God—'X-RAY VICTOR MIKE LOVE—WE HAVE BEEN HIT BY TWO TORPEDOES ... X-RAY VICTOR MIKE LOVE—WE HAVE BEEN HIT BY TWO TOR-PEDOES—NEED IMMEDIATE ASSISTANCE—X-RAY VICTOR MIKE LOVE—WE HAVE BEEN HIT BY TWO TORPEDOES...' Oh, Jesus, God..."*

The man's voice broke completely then. He wept. Sommers cleared his throat, as if he were about to say something, but he remained silent. This went on for several minutes. The man who had been speaking slowly got a hold of himself.

"We were under orders not to break radio silence. We were under orders to deliver the recco team to a position approximately twenty miles off the coast of Hokkaido. We were to rendezvous there with the submarine Chucka, *which then would take the landing party in closer to shore. We obeyed orders. We ignored the SOS. It wasn't until ten days later we learned the CA thirty-five was at the bottom of the Pacific. And more than eight hundred sailors ... Hey, Doc! You're not taping this, are you?"*

From that point on the tape was blank. I rewound it and played it again, and when it was finished, I figured I had what I'd been looking for. It wasn't all of it in place yet. I didn't know what CA 35 meant, and I didn't know the name of the patient, but I was on the threshold of killing. Haywood Sommers and Nikki Scarborough, and tonight, the attempt on Jo. And before them, more than eight hundred sailors. Like the man said, Jesus, God.

Chapter 15———————

The little cases that carry the handguns also carry the rods and wire brushes and solvent and cloth patches to clean them with. So I spread some newspapers atop the kitchen table and cleaned the recently fired .38 caliber Combat Masterpiece that had been built by Mr. Smith and Mr. Wesson and had, along with any number of its brothers, gone off to war with the marines in Korea. And while reaming and swabbing and oiling, I thought about this and that, but the only good that came out of it all, along with a decently cleaned handgun, was remembering that I had told Allison I would call her. I hoped she wasn't asleep. She wasn't.

"You must have been pretty close to the phone."

"I was. I thought you'd call before now."

"I've been making some headway."

"Who with?"

"Jo's at a motel in Salinas. I'm still at the house in Carmel Highlands."

"And I can't get to sleep. Do you really have to spend the night there?"

I thought about it for a moment. "I'm not sure any longer. Somebody telephoned here but hung up after I answered. It might have been Alex, trying to get in touch with Jo, but then again, it might have been the person I'm after, trying to learn if Jo was still here. But since nothing has happened since, maybe the bad guys have closed up shop for the night."

"Then why not come back and hold me, mister." Her voice had a funny tone to it.

"Allison? What's wrong?"

"I don't know. Things don't feel right. I can't explain it. But whenever in the past things haven't felt right, something awful's happened."

"Like what?"

"A death in the family. Something like that."

About twenty seconds went by without either of us speaking. This was brand-new. Allison and I hadn't really spent all that much time together, if the time was measured in days, but the days we had spent together were pretty intense. And we'd spent a few hours on the telephone with each other as well. We were far more than just friends, but in that time, she'd never told me about this side of herself. I thought I was the one who had all the weird hunches.

"Okay, Blondie, sit tight and I'll be back there within twenty minutes. I want to go through the doctor's desk one more time to try and find something."

"Blondie?"

"I'm trying to be funny and flippant. To cheer up my girl friend. You know."

"No, I don't know. Don't ever call me that again. You'll be calling me Cuddles next." She hung up on me.

I went through the doctor's desk. It was a rush job but thorough. After all, I didn't have to worry that the man whose desk I was rifling might come around later and discover somebody had been going through his things. But I still didn't find the code list.

I grabbed the portable tape recorder, the cassette that had the man talking about eight hundred dead sailors and the one that was marked *.30 B M 1919A4*, my toilet kit and gun cases and went back to the motel.

What Allison had in mind was more than holding her. That was after I got even with her for hanging up on me by calling her Cuddles. Once. She in turn immediately got back by giving me an open-handed slap along the side of the head that left my ear ringing. We have a stormy relationship. But we also know how to put that all behind us.

There were times I felt about Allison the way I have felt about no woman since the agonies of first love as a teenage know-nothing. What I felt for her was more than reasonable or safe, and I knew if I ever tried to articulate any of that to her, it might fatally damage whatever it was between us. It certainly was more than a relationship, in the normal sense of the word. A relationship was something I could have on a part-time basis with a smoky number like Jo Sommers. Being with Allison was more like Holy Communion. I was afraid to talk about it and scared to death of losing it. I often wondered if Allison ever felt the same way.

It was something I never could ask her, but later on that night, while I was snuffling in her ear and she was toying with the hair on my chest, I offered an oblique approximation of what I felt for her.

"About a million years ago, you told me that someday you'd like to make yourself a boy child that exhibited some of the same traits that you, at the time, ascribed to me. Remember?"

"The First Night," she intoned. "I remember."

"Still feel that way?"

She rolled onto her stomach, rested her chin on her hands and stared me straight in the eye. "Yup. Someday."

"I know it seems like we've just been through all this, but I'm going to ask again. Would you ever someday consider getting legally hitched to a guy like me and then set about making yourself that male child, or female child, or whatever? I'm not fussy."

"I would seriously consider doing that only when a fellow like you found himself another line of work."

"Oh. That again."

"Yes. That again."

"Well, what if the fellow like me felt he was doing the sort of thing he was meant to be doing, according to some small voice at the very bottom of his existence. Supposing he wouldn't feel right about going into another line of work? What then? Give up on making the boy child?"

"Nope," she said, cocking one elbow to prop up her chin with one hand while her other went exploring. "Seems to me I'd have one of two choices, pardner."

"Such as?"

"I could either find another fellow like you..."

"Or?"

The fingers of her free hand were walking up my leg. "Or I could just go ahead and make me the boy child without bothering to get legally hitched. That way I'd have the boy child and not have to worry all the time about whatever might happen to Papa."

"You really would do that?"

Her fingers quit walking. "Who says I already haven't?"

The next morning, while Allison was in the shower, I replayed the tape about the sailors that I'd listened to the night before. It still didn't trigger any bright ideas. Then I played the other tape, the one with the code that rang faint bells in my memory. And partway through that, the bells clanged.

The patient had been the young marine Billy Carpenter had told me about. He'd been part of the machine-gun squad that was overrun at a river crossing.

The man speaking on the tape was the one who'd
burrowed beneath the bodies of dead marines around
him. The enemy camped around him for the rest of
that night, and the next day they'd carried off their
own dead. That night, the man on the tape had been
able to slip away, back to American lines. But he had
spent something like eighteen hours burrowed beneath the dead bodies of his buddies. It was a
nightmare he had to carry for the rest of his life. Not
even the Silver Star, which he told Sommers he'd
received for that action, could still the memories.

It wasn't a pleasant tale, but by the time I'd heard
most of it, I realized what the tape code was. .30 B M
1919A4. It meant .30-caliber Browning Model 1919A4
machine gun. It would have been the model number
of the machine gun he would have been manning
when his post was overrun. What I remembered was
an obscure bit of knowledge I'd picked up as an
aviation ordnanceman in the navy. Most light machine guns used by American troops in World War
II and Korea were just modifications of the weapon
that John Moses Browning first designed in 1901.
Just after World War I, in 1919, the final modifications were made, creating the weapon used in the
nation's next two major conflicts, the .30-caliber
Browning Models 1919A4 and A6. And that made
me think of something else. Among the models on
the fireplace mantel in the Sommers den was one of
a water-cooled machine gun with its muzzle pointed
groundward. It could have been the doctor's memen-
to of the patient whose story I'd just heard. And the
other cassette codes could be similar, identifying a
piece of ordnance that was a part of the patient's
past. There had to be somebody who could tell me
what CA 35 meant.

I dialed the Wakefield number. While I was waiting for somebody to answer, Allison came out of the

bathroom in her undies. She looked a lot sexier in underwear than Jo Sommers had, but there was no way I could tell her that. She winked at me and went to stand in front of a full-length mirror on the wall and run a brush through her hair.

Mrs. Wakefield answered. I identified myself and asked to speak to her husband. When he came on the line I addressed him as general and told him about the man wearing the cammies who had lobbed a grenade into the Sommers patio the night before. It startled him enough so he told me to call him Gus and asked what he could do for me.

"I think I'm getting close to whatever's behind all this," I told him. "But I need some information. To do with navy things, in World War Two. I'd like to talk to one of your opposite numbers, a navy man, from back in those days. Preferably somebody who doesn't live around here."

"Why not somebody living around here?"

"Because here, I figure, is where the killer lives. And I don't want him to learn how close I am."

He told me to wait a minute. While I waited, I watched Allison step into a pair of blue jeans and a red, turtleneck top. She fussed with her hair some more, then went to the small refrigerator beneath the TV set and poured a couple of glasses of orange juice. Another trait we had in common was that neither one of us ate much of a breakfast, despite what the nutritionists say. You can't let experts run your whole life for you.

"I have the name of a man who should be able to help you," Gus Wakefield's voice said. "If he can't answer your questions, he'll be able to give you the name of somebody who can."

I thanked him and took down the name. It was an Admiral Smith Hollowell, who lived in a suburb of San Diego. I phoned and got the admiral on the line, used Gus Wakefield's name as an introduction, told him about the killings going on hereabouts and the Haywood Sommers tapes.

"What do you need to know?" he barked. He had a high, yappy voice and sounded as if he were late for an appointment.

"I think one of the tapes is a key to all this," I told him. "The patient is talking about something that occurred late in the war. Something like eight hundred sailors dying. It involved a ship identified as CA thirty-five."

"The *Indy*," snapped Hollowell.

"Sir?"

"The cruiser *Indianapolis*. Took two torpedoes, after delivering components of the Hiroshima bomb to Tinian Island. But it wasn't the torpedoes that killed all those bluejackets. It was command failure. Most of those men went mad and drowned. They drifted four days without anybody realizing the ship was missing. Men wearing braid should have been hung for that. And I don't mean the captain of the *Indianapolis*, either. McVay was his name. He committed suicide several years after, you know."

"No, sir, I didn't."

"CA was heavy cruiser designation. The *Indy* was CA thirty-five. You apparently weren't a navy man."

"I was air navy, sir."

"Ah. That explains it. Anything else you need to know?"

"Do you recall if any ships picked up an SOS from the *Indy*, after she was torpedoed?"

"Nobody ever admitted it. But from what *Indy* survivors reported later, they got a message out. And I can't believe every ship and shore station was ignoring guard channels at the time."

"What sort of stir would it cause, this many years

after, if it were revealed somebody had heard the *Indy* signal for help but ignored it?"

Hollowell made something like a dog's growl. "He would be loathed by every man who ever put to sea. Even somebody from air navy should be able to figure that out."

Allison was watching as I hung up the phone. "You learned something big," she told me.

"I learned a part of it," I told her.

"What now?"

"I'm going to go find a library and read about World War Two. What are you going to do?"

"Go paint a picture. Have fun."

Chapter 16

The library in Monterey was on Pacific Street. It had scaffolding along one outer wall. It looked as if workmen were getting ready to build an addition onto it.

The periodical literature guide told me an article about the sinking of the *Indianapolis* had appeared in the August 27, 1945, issue of *Time* magazine. It listed another article that was published in December, 1945, about an inquiry into the sinking.

The twinkly-eyed lady at the information desk told me the library had copies of *Time* magazine on microfilm going back to 1923 and pointed me toward the viewing machine. Five minutes later I was reading about the sinking of the *Indianapolis*. It was a grim account. Hundreds of men had perished as they drifted in the Philippine Sea, hallucinating, dying of shark attack. After that long in the water, life vests became waterlogged, and men had slipped beneath the surface as they scanned the skies and horizon for the help that didn't come until too late, for too many.

The December article quoted testimony by the ship's captain, Charles Butler McVay III. He said he'd been asleep in his sea cabin near the bridge when the torpedoes struck at 12:05 A.M., July 30, 1945. He'd run to the bridge, ordered the navigator to send out a distress call with the ship's position, *"then ran back to his cabin for his clothes."* The article went on to say the loss of the *Indianapolis* produced the heaviest casualty list of any U.S. ship since the battleship *Arizona* was blown apart and sunk at Pearl Harbor.

I wondered why I hadn't remembered something that catastrophic. I'd just been a kid at the time. Maybe the timing had something to do with it. Nuclear weaponry and war's end could shove an item like that right off the front page, and the navy probably hadn't wanted to clang any gongs when it made the announcement of the loss of the *Indianapolis* and a total of 880 crew members.

I thanked the library people for their help and went back across the street to the public parking lot where I'd left my car. It was a nice morning. Sunny and warm. September's a good month in that part of the world. I stood soaking it all in for a minute before getting back in the car.

It seemed to me I had a couple of ways to go about things just then. One would be to take apart the Sommers home until I found the doctor's code list, so I could link a name with the CA 35 tape, or else I could go find young Alex Kilduff and wring his neck until he told me what I wanted to know. I figured it would save time going after Alex.

I drove west, along Lighthouse, then turned onto a street that ran down the long sloping hill not far from Cannery Row. I found the little place Jo had described. It was tucked into a far back corner of a lot with a rickety fence around it. You had to look closely to realize there was a dwelling back there. It was a good spot for a man who enjoyed privacy.

I walked on back and rapped at the front door, then stood to one side so I couldn't be seen through the window in the door. None of that got me anywhere.

Nobody answered the door, and I didn't hear any movement from inside. I walked around the side of the structure, ducking low when I came to a window, just like I was an Indian getting ready to savage the place.

I looked through the window in the back door. I saw only one thing that looked out of place. A light over the kitchen sink was on. I walked back around to the front and looked through another window. It was a little hard to be sure in the daylight, but a lamp in the front room looked as if it were burning as well. At least I didn't see anything that looked like a body.

I walked all around the place again, looking into windows and listening to sirens in the distance. I had never taken a course in locksmithing, so whenever I wanted to get into a place where somebody wasn't holding open the door for me, it was breaking and entering. Things didn't seem to warrant that yet in this instance. Alex was due to show up at the Duck's Quack before long. I'd wait and make a scene there.

I drove back up to Lighthouse and turned east toward the freeway that would carry me over the hill to Carmel, but a block up from Lighthouse I saw cars and wagons blocking the street with their dome lights flashing. I was trying to get to the bottom of something involving two recent murders, a lot of extortion and nearly nine hundred dead sailors from more than three decades earlier. When you're at the edge of that much death, you don't just drive on by and ignore police cars and ambulances clogging a street with emergency lights flashing. I turned and drove up toward the lights. There was a knot of people standing around in a small, municipal park. Somebody was pointing at something at the base of a flagpole. I got out of the car and walked across the street.

Sometimes in a situation like that I cheat a little bit. I carry a plastic enclosed card with a photograph that identifies me as a reporter with the *San Francisco Chronicle*. Media people would have a fit if they knew I was pulling a stunt like that, but the *Chronicle* probably wouldn't much care. I used to be a reporter there, and I still fed them some information from time to time. The bogus card just helped smooth things along with out of town cops. I showed the ID to one of the uniformed officers and asked what was going on.

"Don't know, just got here myself. Speak to the lieutenant in the hat."

He pointed out a short man with no discernible chin who was wearing one of the silver-gray 25th Jazz Festival Anniversary golf caps, like the one Billy Carpenter had been wearing over the weekend. I waited until he'd finished a conversation with a couple of other men. There was what looked like a spattering of dried blood on the pavement at the base of the flagpole, but no body.

The lieutenant turned to me. I showed him the ID and told him I was down there working on a story about the population boom thereabouts and how the old-timers were pulling out their hair over it. Told him I'd seen the flashing lights and decided to stop and see what was going on.

"We're not all that sure yet ourselves what we have," he told me, raising his eyes. "We're just about to get him down. But what it looks like is that somebody shot that gentleman through the head, then looped the flag halyard around his neck and hoisted him up the pole."

That's when I looked up and saw Alex. There was a black hole in the side of his temple and his hands were tied behind his back. A dark scarf had been tied around his eyes, but I could tell it was Alex.

Evidently the cops didn't know him, but they would soon enough if his body had identification on it.

"Hands tied, and blindfolded?" I asked.

"Yeah," said the lieutenant, "almost as if somebody was trying to make a statement. Traitor, comes to mind."

I asked a couple of more questions, making notes in a pad, then told him that either I or a local stringer for the paper would be checking back with him later in the day. Then I got out of there and drove back to the home of the late Alex Kilduff. I parked a block away and hoofed it down the street. This time it didn't have to be breaking and entering, even. A bedroom window at the rear of the house was unlocked. I slid up the sash and boosted myself over the sill.

I went through the place quickly, looking for a desk or some other place where a man would do his paperwork. I figured I would have between ten minutes to a half hour before the police arrived, if they found ID on the body. There wasn't all that much to go through. The bedroom was small and cramped, just room for a double bed, a low cedar chest of drawers and a closet bulging with clothes. If the bedroom was small, the kitchen was an after-thought. It had a refrigerator, a two-burner stove and open shelves that were for the most part bare. The front room took up the rest of the place. There were some books in a bookcase, a portable color television set, one easy chair and a low stand beside it with a telephone atop it. Under the stand was a shoebox where he kept his bills, a legal-sized yellow tablet and an old beer mug stuffed with pencils and ballpoint pens. I sifted through material in the shoebox, but it was mostly bills and circulars. No personal letters, no copies of Dr. Haywood Sommers's audio cassette code.

There was a small writing desk with a floor lamp beside it in a front corner, but the desk held no secrets I was after. The lamp was the one I'd seen through a front window, and I'd been right, it was turned on. It was beginning to look as if somebody had come for young Alex in the night. Or used some ruse to get him out to where somebody was waiting for him.

I crossed to the bookcase. There were some school textbooks in it—American history, theory of economics, a small-business guide and a bunch of paperback science-fiction novels and general fiction. A section of the paperbacks stuck out a little further than the others. I used my handkerchief to pull them out further and found a hardcover book slipped in behind them. I took it out and looked at it and felt myself easing in a little closer to the core of things. It was a volume recently published by Stein and Day, written by a man named Raymond B. Lech. The title was *All the Drowned Sailors.* It was the story of the sinking of the *Indianapolis.*

I backhanded the paperback books into place, but I didn't worry about any fingerprints I might be leaving on the book about the *Indy.* I figured to take it back through the bedroom window with me on my way out. The book would mean more to me than it would to the police. Whenever I got to the bottom of things, I'd let Jo Sommers's lawyer sort it out with the law. I riffled the pages of the book and a photograph fell out of it. It showed a navy enlisted man in working clothes, chambray shirt and dungarees. He was a good-looking young man with a strong resemblance to Alex Kilduff, like an older brother, or his father, maybe. He was seated, half-turned toward the camera and flashing a big grin. From the haircut he wore high on his scalp, it looked as if he'd be Alex's father. And the equipment he was half-turned away from was a ship's radio console. He was what Nikki Scarborough had scribbled shortly before she died. He was a radioman.

I drove several blocks away from there and found a pay phone. I called Jo Sommers to tell her to stay put at the motel. She didn't like that idea, but I told her about what somebody had done to Alex Kilduff, and asked her if she really felt like going back home just then. She allowed as how she didn't.

"Did Alex ever tell you anything about his family?" I asked her.

She thought a moment. "Not that I recall. Why?"

"Did he ever talk about his father, or some other relative being in the navy?"

"No."

"Did he ever say anything about a World War Two cruiser named the *Indianapolis*?"

"No, but ... Hmmmmm."

"What is it?"

"I think there might be a little model of that ship in Woody's den. I think he told me that was the name of it once, when I asked."

I remembered the ship model on the mantel. "You could be right. I'm still looking for the code list for the tapes. What sort of paper was it on?"

She said the list was in a small, black spiral binder that looked like an address book. I told her it would have helped if she'd thought to tell me that earlier.

I got back on the freeway, went over the hill and turned off to go into Carmel. I found a parking place a half block up from the Duck's Quack, fed the parking meter and went down to where they were expecting Alex to show up and open the bar. When I squinted through a front window, I saw a woman carrying a clipboard inventorying the liquor in the bottles on the back bar. I rapped on the window and grinned and made funny faces until she knew I wasn't going to go away until the place opened. She came to the front door and opened it with a little smile.

"In case you couldn't tell from the outward signs, we aren't opened yet."

She was a woman with a small but trim build. She was about five feet tall, had a medium-sized chest and a meaty pair of hips she kept under tight control in denim. Black hair fell down her back. She was wearing a thin, filmy white blouse and had neglected to put on her bra that morning.

"I got the outward signs," I told her. "I also have some inside information you'll want me to share. You the owner?"

"No, but the boss tells me I'm one helluva manager. Is the information important to me and the job?"

"Downright crucial, at this given moment."

"Well then. Maybe you'd best step inside."

She held open the door and I went in. The place had the sort of smells even the best run bars have before they open the doors and give it a chance to air out.

She closed the door again and went over behind the bar. "My name's Dee," she said. "Want a cup of coffee?"

"My name's Pete, and I'd love some coffee."

She poured out a couple of cups from a pot on a two-burner hot plate next to a blender. "Cream or sugar?"

"Both."

She doctored it up with a professional flourish and slid the cup onto the bar in front of me. She drank her own coffee black. It matched the color of her eyes. She put her cup on the bar next to mine, then came around and climbed atop a stool beside me and tucked her feet beneath her, Indian fashion.

"You're a handsome dog," she said with a little giggle, taking a sip of the coffee. "I saw you stick your head in here briefly the other night. You had a gorgeous blonde with you. That your wife?"

"Nope. She's my number one girl friend, but we live a couple of hundred miles apart, so most of our conversation's over the telephone. We came down for the jazz festival. And thanks for the compliment. You're pretty cute yourself. If the gorgeous blonde wasn't still down here with me, I'd probably try to see what sort of trouble I could get into with you. If any."

"That might be fun," she told me. "I've been here five years now, and I don't have any plans to leave. You might stop by sometime when you're in town without the gorgeous blonde. Where are you from?"

"San Francisco."

"That's close enough so you could come down almost any weekend at all."

"That was going around the back of my own head."

She had a laugh in the high octaves and an inviting look on her small, angular face that made me wish I wasn't working. Then she had another sip of her coffee and voiced my own feelings.

"But then, we can't just sit here and bullshit away the rest of the morning, can we? You were going to tell me something."

"Yes. I have good news and bad news."

"Doesn't everybody. This day's already off to a rocky start. Good news first, please."

"Your bar is going to get some sensational publicity in the *Monterey Herald* tomorrow morning."

"Oh, that's nice. You sure?"

"It's guaranteed."

"What sort of sensational publicity?"

"That's the bad news."

"Which is?"

"Alex isn't going to make it in to work this morning."

"Damn it," she said, with another sip of the coffee. "I might have known."

"How's that?"

"It's the streak I've been on lately. It means I'll have to work the day shift myself, and I had a luncheon date with a nice-looking boy who's new to the area."

"Is that why you left your bra at home this morning?"

It got another of the high-register laughs. "You're observant."

"You bet."

"Why isn't Alex going to make it to work this morning? You a friend of his?"

"Nope. He wouldn't let me get that close to him. And the reason he isn't going to make it to work is the really bad part of the bad news."

The glitter went out of her face and she set the coffee aside. She was quick and bright. And ready.

"Before I tell you," I began, "I have to ask you a really important favor. Like forgetting we had this conversation when the cops come around."

"Oh-oh. It really is bad news, then."

"Very bad."

She made a little face and nodded. "I can probably do you that favor without much trouble. It'd be even easier if I thought you'd really come back down here some weekend without another woman on your arm."

"It's a promise."

"Before too many years go by."

"Before even the rest of this year goes by."

She put out a small hand with a good grip to it when we shook. "Call a couple of days ahead," she told me, "so I can cancel all my other social engagements."

I smiled and took out a business card and handed it to her. "If you get to San Francisco before I get back down here, you can give me a call. You don't even have to call a couple of days ahead of time."

"You don't have any San Francisco girl friends?"

"Not really. I keep pretty busy most of the time."

She was reading the card and made a little humming noise. "I suppose this is why you don't want me to tell the cops about the conversation we're having."

"That's right. I'm working, and while I've had some dealings with the local law, I'm not ready just yet to tell them everything I've got. I have a client who could be in very serious trouble if the cops knew the things about her and Alex that I know."

She looked at me sharply. "Who's the client?"

"Jo Sommers. Her husband, a retired psychiatrist, was murdered Friday night. Know her?"

"No, but I read about him, of course. I mean the murder."

"There have been a couple of other killings since then, all a part of the same business."

"Alex?"

"The most recent. And most spectacular. That's why you're going to get the sensational publicity."

She had another sip of coffee. "Tell me about it."

So I told her about the flagpole. Her eyes widened some, and when I'd finished telling her, she shook her head.

"Dynamite way to go," she said.

"I'll bet he thought so."

She giggled again.

"The two of you couldn't have been too close," I said.

"We weren't."

"Any special reason?"

She held one hand out and wagged it from side to side. "He was just a little too precious. Too glib, too friendly. Too—too bubbly. Myself, I don't particularly care for that in a man. I mean, I don't think you have to be all strong and silent, bordering on glum or anything. But then, I don't think you have to be out there dancing on tiptoes all the time, either."

It was my turn to chuckle. I had some of the coffee. I felt this was the sort of lady a guy like me could trust. Far more than I ever could trust a woman like Jo Sommers.

"So now if I've got your promise you won't tell the cops I've been here this morning..." I told her.

"Cross my heart." She clamped one hand across her right breast with a saucy grin.

"Then I'll tell you what I really came by to ask. I need to know anything you can tell me about Alex. Where he's from. How I might be able to get in touch with his family. I'd like to be able to do that before the cops do."

Dee put down the coffee and slid off the stool. "I don't know that," she told me, "but I might have a way of finding out."

I got up and followed her. She led me down a hallway past the restrooms and unlocked the door to a little office. She rummaged around in a desk drawer and took out a small white card with some numbers on it. Then she led me back to a room where they stored soft drinks and had a big machine that made ice cubes. There also were several lockers in there with combination locks on them. She went over to one of them, consulted the card and spun the combination dial. A moment later she popped open the locker drawer.

"Aren't I wonderful," she said, turning with a grin. Hanging inside the locker was a pair of dark trousers and a couple of shirts. Dee reached in and took a small carton down from an upper shelf. "Mail call," she told me, handing it to me.

"What's this?"

"Mail. He got all his mail here. Even local bills."

"He didn't get home delivery?"

"I don't know. Maybe he could have, but that would have meant letting people know where he lived. He was a little funny that way. You can bring that back and use the desk in the office, if you'd like. I've got to get back to work, especially since I have to open the place."

In five minutes I had what I wanted. I found two letters from the same town back in Pennsylvania. One was from a girl, the other was filled with family gossip and signed, "Mom." I copied the return address on the envelope from Mom then took the carton back and shut up the locker.

When Dee unlocked the front door for me, I thanked her with a wink and said I'd see her later. She winked back and said she hoped so.

I stopped at another pay phone on my way back to the car and called the motel Allison and I were staying at. I asked the man on the switchboard to try ringing our room. He did, but there was no answer.

"But somebody's been calling for you," he told me. "Some fellow. A couple of times, now."

"Did he leave a message?"

"He just said he had something important to tell you."

"Did he leave a number?"

"No, he just said he'd call back."

Chapter 17 ─────────

I thanked him and hung up. On the way back to the car I thought about things. Despite his public life at the Duck's Quack, Alex seemed to have lived cautiously. Probably because he'd been planning a major bit of blackmail to do with the sinking of the *Indianapolis* for a good long while, maybe even before he came to Carmel, from some of the things Jo Sommers had told me, and from what the book and photograph I'd lifted out of his bookcase would indicate.

But he hadn't been careful enough to prevent somebody from putting a bullet through his head and hanging him out to dry atop the flagpole. And I hadn't been making any secret of what I'd been doing since the weekend, and if anybody was interested in what I was doing, they'd also be interested in the fact that I had my girl friend with me. I decided it was time to put Allison on a plane and get her out of there. She'd have to learn if she could live with the rigors of my job another time.

I drove down past the motel and turned onto Scenic Road, where we'd taken our morning walks. I stopped and got out a couple of times to scan the beach below me, but I didn't see the kid in blue jeans and red turtleneck top. Then I thought of something. She'd told me that morning she was going to go paint a picture. And the day before, when I'd shown her the Stilwell house, she'd told me she'd sketch it for me someday. Maybe she was up there now, doing one or the other.

I drove over to Inspiration Road. At the Stilwell home, Inspiration forms the top part of a T with San Antonio Road, and I figured that down San Antonio a ways is where somebody would set up things to best sketch the house. I didn't see Allison. I drove slowly along the road, looking at things. I was thirty yards back from Inspiration Road when I saw something that made me hit the brakes and jump out of the car. Allison's sketchpad was lying facedown on the tree-shaded, dirt and grass parking strip alongside the road. I picked up the pad and looked at it. I'd been right. She'd made some tentative outlines of the house down the way. A few feet away I found a couple of the sketching pencils she used. I put these things in my car and studied the ground around me some more. Some trampling had gone on there. In the dry dirt I could make out a gridmark that looked like the waffle pattern left by a hiking boot. There also was a single strand of blonde hair, that could have been from the head of my lady. I looked for tire treads at the edge of the roadway but didn't see any. Then I began to knock on doors.

An elderly man with a slight stoop and a pipe in his hand answered the door behind the hedge where I'd found the sketchpad. He'd seen Allison there earlier. He'd been outside watering his lawn and had seen her settling down with her sketchpad. She had a grand smile, he told me. He said they'd chatted pleasantly for a minute, then he'd gone on about his chores and finally went back inside the house. No, he wasn't able to see her from inside the house. And no, he didn't hear any commotion outside afterward. No raised voices or squeal of tires.

Across the street a stout woman wearing a yellow housecoat with curlers in her hair and holding a calico cat to her chest answered my knock. She hadn't seen nor heard anything unusual. At three other homes in the area, two of the residents weren't any help. But the third, a retired gentlemen in his early sixties, had noticed Allison sketching when he drove into his driveway after a trip to the market.

It was a gray-haired woman, thin as a stick, pruning her hedge two homes further up the block, who was able to give me the story of what had happened, about forty minutes earlier. She'd been inside her yard working when a noise that seemed unusual prompted her to go to the front gate and look down the street. A woman wearing a red top was either being helped or shoved into the back of an automobile by a man wearing some sort of uniform.

"You know, like they wear in the army these days." She had a slow, deliberate manner of speaking.

"Camouflage material, you mean."

"Yes, I guess that's what it was."

"Did the woman seem to be struggling?"

"I couldn't tell that. She was partway into the back of the car when I saw them. I had the impression somebody else was already in the back of the car. Then the man with the uniform shut the door, got into the front and drove off."

"Did they drive past here?"

"No, they went on up the street in the other direction and turned the corner left."

"Do you remember what the car looked like?"

"Oh, I'm afraid not. So many of them look so much alike these days, don't you think? It was a dark color. Dark blue, or black, maybe."

"What sort of sound was it that made you come to the gate?"

"I don't really know. Either—well, I couldn't tell if

it was human or animal, to tell you the truth. Kind of a whoop. Or a cry, maybe."

We talked for a moment more and I went back to the car, then just sat there, staring through the windshield without seeing anything. I'd wised up too late, that was the dominating thought. The rest was a jumble. My mind was going on in a dozen different directions, and it took a major effort to calm down. The man at the motel said somebody had called me. Maybe it was somebody who knew about Allison. I drove back there.

Up in the room I sat and thought about how easy it would have been for somebody to get a line on me and have the motel under observation. I hadn't been secretive about what I'd been doing, and when they saw me go off by myself that morning, they could have waited until Allison came out, followed her and set up the snatch.

The phone rang twenty minutes later. It was a flat, male voice that I didn't recognize.

"We have your woman," he said dryly. "We want you out. Out of town, out of this part of the state. We don't want you back. Just drop what you're doing. You'll be under surveillance. We'll know whether or not you leave. After you've been gone for two days, we'll release the woman. She was blindfolded, so she can't identify us. We have no cause to fear or harm her. So in two days we'll release her. Pack up and leave."

"After I talk to the woman you took."

"What?"

"Bring her to the phone and let me speak with her. If you have harmed her, or cause her any harm at any time, I might as well let you know this. I'll kill you. I'll find and kill you and anybody else who's a part of this. You had better believe I can do that. I could give you references."

He didn't reply right away. "She's not where she can come to the phone," he said finally. "It would take a little while to arrange that."

"I'll be right here."

"All right. We'll get back to you as soon as we can. Only hear this. Don't make any attempt to arrange to have the call traced when we bring her to a phone. It will be a very brief call. Just long enough so you can know she's all right."

He hung up.

I replaced the receiver and did a little pacing around the room, trying to pretend Allison was somebody else's girl. That it was just a job, like any other job, to find her and to get her out of the trouble she was in. Be cold and disassociate, I told myself. I worked on that for a couple of minutes or longer, until I felt I was far enough back from it to make decisions that had to be made.

I telephoned directory assistance in the small Pennsylvania town on the return address of the envelope from Alex's mother. Using the last name and street address, I was able to get the phone number. I dialed it, but nobody answered. I hung up and began to pack.

I phoned the desk and asked them to have my bill ready, that we were checking out. When I was finished packing and had made a final check of the room, I put the luggage over by the door, then sat down by the window and stared out at the trees across the street and the water beyond. And I thought some pretty awful thoughts.

The phone rang a half hour later. Allison was on the line when I answered.

"Pete?"

"Are you all right?"

"I guess . . . I got shoved around some. And they

have something tied around my eyes. But I guess I'm okay."

"Did they—"

But the flat male voice came on the line then. "Get out of town," he said and hung up.

I settled up at the motel office, put the luggage in the car and drove over to the highway. I made one stop, at a pay phone, and called Jo Sommers. I told her I wouldn't be in touch for a while, but she was to stay where she was until she heard from me again. I told her it could be for as long as a day or two. She began to chatter, but I cut her off and hung up, then got in the car and headed north.

When the road widened into a freeway again at the top of the hill, I traveled at a steady 55 miles an hour. I began watching traffic around and behind me.

I was on a stretch of road that passed through Fort Ord, home of the 7th Infantry Division. There were rifle ranges off to my left, built into the high, buff-colored sand dunes along Monterey Bay. I had read recently that they were planning to trim the 7th from its normal complement of fourteen thousand men to a lighter-weight ten-thousand-man, quick-reaction strike division. Lean and mean and quick.

I remembered Allison when she had made the lightning sketch of the trees and water below the motel room. She had pumped enormous concentration into just a few moments of marking on paper and created a scenic wonder. That was the nub of her reservations about hanging out with me. She could only work the way she did by that sort of concentration, and the freedom from worry that made it possible.

I stared at the rearview mirror, ticking off the cars I'd seen since leaving Carmel. Making note of the additions, watching for signs of erratic position changes.

I left behind the plains and dunes of Fort Ord and drove past artichoke fields. Four miles further along, Highway 1 pinched down from a freeway to a two-lane highway. Some of the traffic behind me turned off onto Highway 156, leading to Castroville and Prunedale. I continued up Highway 1, past the big steam-generating plant at Moss Landing to the right, and a rambling yard where they sold Mexican pottery on my left.

Allison had told me she wanted to stop at the pottery lot on our way home. It was the sort of thing she liked to do, window shopping, mostly. She seldom bought things but liked to stroll around the rows of pots and dishes and statues, a little frown pinching her forehead, concentrating on the designs. She called it idea shopping. Out of the blue I got a lump in my throat. I squeezed the steering wheel and studied the traffic behind me.

At 21.7 miles north of Carmel I passed a Fast Gas station. Next to it was a little shop called Military Collectibles. I had been coming down to the Monterey area for a dozen years. Each time, I told myself, I'd have to stop in there and see what sort of military collectibles they had. Medals and helmets and belt buckles and division patches, would be my guess. I wondered if they stocked any cammies.

I wondered something else, as well. I wondered who all of us thought we were kidding. They hadn't bought themselves a couple of days by taking Allison. They'd bought themselves a couple of hours.

At 22.8 miles north of Carmel I passed Leoninie's Fruit Stand. The highway widened again ahead of me into a divided freeway, and I gradually increased my speed. I kept increasing it until I was moving along at 80 miles an hour. The closest traffic behind me was back a mile or more. At 27.9 miles and 35 minutes out of Carmel, I shot off Highway 1 onto Airport Boulevard in Watsonville.

I parked and locked the car in a lot behind a small general aviation office. I traveled light. I had my toilet kit, the .38 revolver and the .45 automatic along with spare ammunition. I left the luggage in the car. I went into the office and told a sandy-haired fellow behind the desk I wanted to hire me a plane and pilot for a flight to the Monterey County Airport.

"It's an emergency," I told the man. "I need to be there ten minutes ago."

He put aside a pipe and got up to walk past me and stick his head out the door. He called for somebody named Chuck. Ten minutes later Chuck and I had reached the high point of a parabolic curve we flew between the two airports and began our landing glide.

I had paid for the flight before we took off. When we landed at Monterey, he taxied over toward the terminal building and I got out.

I went to a phone booth and called my office in San Francisco. Ceejay answered, and I told her somebody had abducted Allison. It cut the legs out from under the small talk.

"Tell me what you want," she said grimly.

"I want you to call Turk Connell at World Investigations. Tell him what happened and tell him I want at least two men—up to four, if he can spare them. Tell them they have to be men willing to harm other men, if it comes to that. He'll know that, but tell him anyhow. If he can spare only two men, tell him to start them on their way to Monterey. By the time they get here and find a pay phone, I'll have called their office and told them where I'm staying. If he can spare three or four men, send one of them down to Salinas. When that man gets there, he's to phone back to the office for instructions, same as the others."

"Got it."

I thought a moment more. "Then see if you can get in touch with John Foley at the Hall of Justice. Tell him what happened, and say it would be nice if he left word where he'll be until this is all over with, in case I get into trouble with the local cops and need a reference. I guess that's it, Ceejay. I have to go find a motel room and think about things. I'll let you know where I am when I'm settled."

"Pete?"

"Yes?"

"I'm in for the duration."

"How do you mean?"

"I'll be here in the office, at the phone, until this is over. Tonight, tomorrow, next week, whenever."

"That shouldn't be necessary, Ceejay. We have a good answering service."

"I know. But I'm going to be here. Take care of yourself, and get that girl back."

Her voice was a little choked up. I knew how she felt. She'd told me once that taking up with Allison was the only really bright thing she'd ever known me to do. I went over to the rental car counter.

Chapter 18 ─────────────

World Investigations was, for my money, about the slickest operation around these days. They weren't as big as Pinkerton's, but they were large enough to have agents in offices throughout major cities in this country, Europe and parts of Asia. When they needed more manpower, they signed on local investigators for short-term duty. In San Francisco, I was one of the people they called in when they needed to swell the ranks. And they were the people I went to when I needed backup. They were, for the most part, a daring bunch of scalawags intent on getting the job done.

The two operatives Turk Connell sent me were named Collins and Reinhardt. Collins was a medium-built man so bland-looking he could blend into the wall behind him. He wore rimless glasses but said they were just a part of his cover. Reinhardt looked the way his name sounded, like a Teutonic beer salesman. He was big and stout with an oversized baby face. But I'd seen Reinhardt in action. He looked like an oaf, but he was sly and could move like the wind.

We met at the motel I'd checked into just off the freeway in Monterey. They told me a third man would be on his way to Salinas late that afternoon. A fourth man would be on his way down as well the next morning. I told the two men everything except the specific role Jo Sommers had played in the extortion racket that was behind it all. I just told them that my client had participated in some illegalities I didn't want the local cops to find out about. They took it all in with a shrug. Good men.

I'd found myself using the word *racket* when I mentioned the extortion operation. I'd never associated the word *racket* with what Jo had been a part of until just then. But that's what it was. The woman just had a way of talking a man out of his britches and all good sense along with it. Maybe it took what happened to Allison for me to be able to see it all a little more clearly.

"What sort of idiot would go around doing this kind of shit wearing cammies?" Reinhardt asked of nobody in particular.

"The sort who runs a personal ad in *Soldier of Fortune* magazine offering to go anywhere and do anything," said Collins.

I looked up at him and blinked. "I think you two have already earned your fee."

They frowned back at me.

"I'll bet that's exactly the sort of man we're looking for. And that could be where the man behind it all went to find somebody to do his killing. It had never occurred to me."

"You've had other things on your mind," said Reinhardt. "The thing is now, how do we go about finding the right balls to kick?"

"I've thought about that some," I told them. "From the conversation I had with the man on the phone, it's set up so they only have two days. The deal was, they were to release Allison by then. If they did release her and she went on home, there would be nothing to keep me from coming back down here to finish whatever I was doing before. And they sure as hell know I'd be down here like a shot if they didn't release Allison when they said they would. So whatever they want to do, they figure they can accomplish in a couple of days. I think they plan to find and snuff Jo Sommers, or do something at the Sommers home, or both."

I turned to Reinhardt. "I think you should get on over to the motel in Salinas and cover Jo until the next man gets down here. There's no reason they should know where she is, but she's an unpredictable woman, and she might have gotten lonely and started to telephone friends to pass the time.

"I want Collins to help me get into the Sommers home without anybody knowing I got in there, then he can come back here and try to reach that number in Pennsylvania. What we're looking for is the name of the skipper or the executive officer of the ship Alex's father was serving on in the last days of World War Two. I assume it was his father. Mrs. Kilduff should be able to tell us. Or maybe the man himself will answer the phone."

"If I can't raise somebody soon," said Collins, "how about I try to get somebody out of our Scranton office to shag on over there and track down people."

"Fine idea."

"Or I could just give it all to Scranton and come join you at the Sommers home," he suggested.

"No, until we get a little more depth, you're better off here. When the man with cammies shows up, I want you to be available as backup in either direction. I've lost him twice. I don't want to lose him again. It's one of the reasons I called you people. And killing the son of a bitch won't be good enough. We've got to shake him until he tells us things. If he shows up at the Sommers house, you can be there inside of seven minutes. If it's Salinas, you can make it in under twenty. That's a long time, but I have faith in your partner. Did you bring hand radios?"

Reinhardt nodded. "But you might as well take mine. They won't have Salinas range."

"Okay, but I'll only use it to goose Collins if the man in the cammies shows up. If either of you want to talk to me, ring the Sommers home twice, hang up and call back. I'm not taking any other calls."

"Sounds good," said Reinhardt. "You want a pump?"

"What?"

"I've got a shotgun in the car. You want it?"

"No, I might hit our man in the throat with something like that. Just remember. Right now we're not concerned about extortion or wartime heroics. We just want Allison. Period."

I phoned Jo and told her about Reinhardt and that he'd be checking into a motel unit near her own. She started to complain about it, so I told her about Allison. She was smart enough to shut up after that.

Reinhardt took off for Salinas, and Collins and I drove up to a large shopping center. I waited in the car while he went in and bought us both some dark work clothes. He changed into his in the car while I drove us over to a truck rental place. Collins went in and filled out the forms to lease a small, enclosed moving van. I showed him on a map how to get to the street the Sommers home was on and gave him the address.

I climbed into the back of the van. Collins closed the door and drove us on out to Carmel Highlands, backed into the driveway of the Sommers home, used the key I'd given him to let himself in the front door and went around to open the garage door. Then he opened the rear doors of the van and clamped them back flat against the sides of the truck. He got back into the cab and backed the van up right to the garage entrance. I stepped out of the van into the garage. Collins followed.

The cat was waiting and yowling. I fed it, then showed Collins through the place, so he'd know the layout if he had to come back on business. I changed into the dark clothes while Collins got a beer out of the refrigerator and went into the front room to keep an eye on the van and make sure nobody came nosing around it. He also found a phone jack in there, so he got the phone out of the study to make a couple of calls. He still couldn't get an answer at the Kilduff home in Pennsylvania, so he called the World Investigations office in Scranton and arranged for somebody to hustle over to Alex's hometown.

When Collins had finished his beer, he went back out and went through the rigmarole of moving the van away from the garage door, closing it up, then closing the garage door and locking it from inside.

"Drive around some to make sure nobody's interested in your load," I told him on his way back through the house.

"Right. I'll call when I get back to the motel."

He drove off and I began taking apart the house, looking for the spiral address book with a black cover. It was a long afternoon. The phone rang a couple of times, but not with the prearranged double ring. I kept on searching. I learned quite a bit about the personal life of Haywood Sommers and his wife Jo, but I didn't find the address book until it was nearly dark out. I had moved out to the garage and used my penlight to begin going through the cartons up in the storage loft among the rafters. The spiral pad was on top of the tapes in the easiest carton to get to. I took it back inside the house proper to a corner of the doctor's den and went through it page by page. While I was doing that the phones went off again. They rang twice and fell silent. I'd brought the phone Collins had used back to the den. When it rang again I answered.

It was Reinhardt, with some disappointing news. "The man who was coming down here is delayed. He might not make it until ten or eleven tonight."

"That means you'll have to stick there. Do you have a good vantage point?"

"Yeah. The units are in a U-shape. I'm at the top of one of the legs. She's partway down the side opposite me. I can keep an eye on her roofline, the courtyard and whoever drives in. The place is well lighted. I'm set."

"Okay. You'd better let Collins know you're sticking."

"I will. I was just talking by phone with the lady. She's bitching about wanting to go out for some hot food."

"Tell her to phone some place that delivers. She stays put."

"Right."

I hung up and went back to the spiral address book. Partway through it, something became apparent. I wasn't going to find the name I wanted. A few of the names had been heavily scored out, so I couldn't read them. One of the blacked-out names was opposite the code designation CA 35. There were other names throughout the book that hadn't been scored out, but I didn't find the name Wakefield, nor Larry Pitt. The doctor must have crossed out the names of former patients, or in Gus Wakefield's case, the brother, who lived in the Monterey area. He would remember them well enough, since he traveled in their circles, and it must have struck him as a bit of ethical courtesy to strike those names to safeguard the rough parts of his neighbors' pasts.

But then, I wondered, how did Alex manage to identify them? I studied the blacked out names closer and figured I had the answer. Alex had seen the book before the names were crossed out. The ink that scored the names was a brighter hue than that of the other writing in the book. Sommers probably had crossed them out after Alex had put the extortion program into operation, after Billy Carpenter had given him hell thinking Sommers was behind the extortion attempts.

I put the address book back into the doctor's desk. The phones rang again, steadily. I prowled around the darkened home. I was getting tired of the place. I was tired of nothing happening. Even the cat had left. I phoned Collins back at the motel to see if anything was going on.

"Things are still quiet in Salinas," he told me. "Reinhardt's relief still hasn't shown up. I haven't heard back from the Scranton office, and here I sit."

"Yeah. Me too."

I hung up and decided I didn't have to sit right there inside the house all the time. In fact a patrol of the perimeter fence would properly be in order, so long as I didn't terrify the neighbors. I had the impression that outside of the sound of fire trucks or grenades going off, the neighbors kept pretty much to themselves.

I slipped out the patio door and pulled it shut behind me. I ambled around the patio, peering through the bougainvillea and listening to the night. It was noisy. The air was clear as a bell and the booming of the surf on the distant beach carried through the night like artillery fire. It would have been hard to hear the fall of a softly shod foot. I went through the lattice gate beyond the hot tub and prowled the backyard. The house in back was dark. I went to the corner of the house and took a look down the side where the ice plant grew. I turned and strolled back to the other corner and was about to round it when I heard something that made me stop

in my tracks. The surf might have covered the sound
of a footfall, but not the tinkle of glass. I got down
on my haunches and took a peek around the corner.
A dark figure had placed a short ladder against the
side of the house. He was atop the ladder, reaching
through the hole he'd just punched in the window to
unlock and open the window in Jo's bedroom. He
was over the windowsill and inside before I could
think what to do. He had a flashlight with him and
was flashing it around the bedroom. He closed what
was left of the window and the room went dark.

I trotted around to the front of the house. The
bobbing flash was in the front room now, just briefly.
He wanted to make sure nobody was home. There
was a three-quarter-ton stake truck backed up in the
driveway I hadn't heard. Probably because of the
distant surf. Either the man in the house had put it
there or somebody who might have come with him.
The angle wasn't right for me to see into the truck
cab. I stayed put a couple of minutes to see if
anybody else was going to get out of the truck. When
the man inside opened the garage door, I edged
back around the corner, swung myself again over the
warped gate and went around to the backyard and
through the patio gate. I eased open the sliding glass
doors. The door from the kitchen into the garage
was slightly ajar, and a light came from the garage
itself. I could hear grunts and some sort of sliding
noises from in there. I glided down the carpeted
hallway to the doctor's study, where I'd left the hand
radio.

It was time to get Collins moving, but a scraping
sound along the side of the house made me hesitate.
The man was already taking away the ladder he'd
used to get up to the window in the bedroom next to
the study. I didn't take a chance on using the radio.
I carried it into the front room and stood well back

from the windows. The man was putting the ladder onto the bed of the truck. He was a fast worker. Half a dozen cartons already were loaded onto the truck bed, near the back of the cab. They looked like the cartons the audio cassettes had been in up in the garage loft. He must have gotten them down from there before he'd opened the garage door, while I was hunkered down waiting to see if anybody was with him.

He went into the garage again and closed the door. If he was getting ready to leave, I didn't have time to use the radio or telephone or anything else. The first thing I had to do was hide.

I ducked into Jo's bedroom, crossing to open the door to the walk-in closet. I stepped inside and nestled myself among the frills and flounces and slid the door mostly closed. I heard the door from the kitchen to the garage close. He came walking back through the house, flashing his light here and there as he moved. When he passed the open bedroom door I could hear him whistling softly between his teeth. He paused and flashed the light briefly over the broken window, then continued on to the front of the house. The front door opened and closed. I got hung up on something lacy while I was trying to get out of the closet and use the radio at the same time. Something ripped and came off a hanger, clinging to my elbow as I stumbled into the bedroom.

"Collins, this is Bragg, do you read me?" I shook off whatever was clinging to my arm and headed for the front door. Outside the truck engine started. "Collins, do you read me?"

There was some crackle and static from the little speaker. By the time I cracked open the front door, the man in the truck had already rolled out of the driveway and headed off down the street. I bellowed a curse. I was going to lose him again. I pitched the radio onto the nearby sofa and went out the door.

One thing, at least, the man in the truck didn't seem to know. There was just one street that led out of this small community to Highway 1, Ribera Road. It made a long, deep loop around the perimeter of the area. He was taking the long way. There was just a chance I could intercept the truck by cutting across the street above the Sommers home and intercepting Ribera a couple of blocks over. There was only one way to make that work. I had to run like hell. I ran.

Chapter 19 ──────────

I don't like running all that much. It hadn't bothered me so much when I was a kid, growing up. In fact I'd had some deviltry in me, growing up, and there were times when running for my life was the only thing that kept me from packing home a black eye at day's end. But since those days I'd grown and filled out enough so that extended running was a job. And add to that the odd bullet-wound scar here, the once-fractured bone there, and it all came together to remind me of my spotty past when I had to run that way. Then there was the weaponry. I had the .38 revolver on my right hip and the .45 automatic in the shoulder holster under the dark windbreaker Collins had bought me. The revolver wasn't much of a problem, except for the additional weight, but the .45 was a handicap. If I'd known I was going to be in a footrace with a stake truck, I would have strapped the holster tighter around my chest. As it was, it thumped and bumped in counterpart to pounding heart beneath it. But I wasn't about to throw either of the guns away. One thing I did have to do was to transfer a spare magazine for the .45 and a box of .38 shells for the revolver from the windbreaker pockets into my trousers so they wouldn't bounce out. Finally, though, when the pain began to get to me, I thought about Allison. That put most other things out of my mind.

I got to the corner of Meadow Way and Ribera about ten seconds ahead of the truck. I knelt gasping for breath inside a nearby hedged driveway. At least the truck wasn't moving so fast that I risked killing myself trying to get aboard. It chugged on by and I ran out and caught the slats along the side opposite the drive. Pulling myself up over the side was painful and time-consuming, but by the time we reached Highway 1, I was aboard and hunkered down up against the cab, where I couldn't be seen in the side or rearview mirrors. At Highway 1, the driver turned right and headed south. I stared at the stars and got my breath back.

He took a while to get to where we were going. I hoped, of course, that we were going to wherever they had Allison. But we weren't. Where he was headed for, it turned out, was a convenient place to dump the cartons of audio cassettes, where hopefully the stuff of extortion would be forever cast out to sea. If I'd known that was what he was looking for, I could have knocked on the back of the cab and suggested several other places along the coast road dug into the high cliffs. Maybe he was a stranger to the area and had been given specific instructions about where to dump them. At any rate, the place he chose was a spectacular bridge spanning a gorge several miles south of Carmel.

The first inkling I had of what he was up to was when he pulled off to the side of the road to let a car about a quarter mile behind us go past. Then he drove out onto the two-lane bridge, swung across the centerline and stopped. He put the truck into reverse and backed up to the guard railing.

By the time he'd started to back up, I was over the side and crouched down low. This was a long, naked bridge, a couple of hundred feet over a river pouring into the Pacific Ocean below us. It wasn't a good place to play hide-and-go-seek. I did not intend to go over the railing and see if there was something to hang from beneath the roadbed. When the truck stopped, I rolled beneath it. The man inside opened the door and climbed up into the truck bed. There was grunting and scraping again as he lifted the cartons and hurled them over the railing into the water below.

A moment later he was clambering back down into the cab, and I was rolling out from beneath the truck on the opposite side. When the door banged shut, I got up and grabbed the slats again as the truck began to move and made a wide loop to head back north. I lifted my legs to keep from losing them as he banged off the opposite railing. By the time I got back up over the side of the truck, I was panting and my heart was thumping once again. It took a few miles before I calmed down.

He drove north of the Carmel exits this time and turned onto the road that dips down into Pacific Grove and the butterfly trees. And it was almost to the butterfly trees that we traveled, down past the entrance to the Del Monte property with the swank homes and the slick golf courses where they hold the Crosby Pro-Am Tournament, almost to the ocean itself. But he turned finally onto Asilomar Avenue and drove north, past the conference grounds. Then he slowed and stopped, in the middle of the road. Off to the right was a large old, three-story home glowing with lights and rattling with laughter and conversation. We'd come to a party, and the man in the cab hadn't expected that. Cars were parked in the driveway and lined both sides of the road. He put the truck back into gear and moved ahead slowly, looking for a parking place. When he found a big enough gap between cars he braked again, I went over the side, and he backed into the open space. I lost myself in the shadows of nearby cars, and made my way back toward the house. I scrunched down beside some trees next to the driveway. I had my first clear view of the man in the truck when he swung down out of the cab and approached the house. He was wearing a camouflage uniform, minus the duckbill cap. He'd probably fit right in at the party. Cammies were a fashionable item this year. They had designer cammies for smart women and dumb kids.

The truck driver went up to the front door, rang the bell and rapped on the side molding. He didn't seem to be all that learned about house parties and other urban affairs. Maybe he'd spent the last few years out in the South African bush or in Central America.

He wised up eventually and opened the door and stuck his head inside long enough to ask for somebody, then he backed off and took a turn around the front porch, staring out at the truck. He was about six feet tall with a medium build and a meaty, pitted face, as if he'd had a bad case of acne when he was young. His eyes seemed to bug out of his face a little. He had thinning dark hair and a nervous habit of hunching his shoulders. I'd seen that in men who'd been subjected to severe shell fire. I estimated his age to be in the early thirties.

The door opened again and a man stepped out onto the porch. He was wearing dark slacks and a white turtleneck sweater. I recognized him. And I assumed he was the man on the tape, the skipper who'd ignored the SOS from the *Indianapolis*. It was one of the men Billy Carpenter had introduced me to at the Hunt Club the night Haywood Sommers was smothered to death. I'd seen him the next night as well, at the Gus Wakefield party, talking to Lawrence Pitt. Whiteman was his name. They called him Whitey, and Wakefield told me he'd captained a destroyer in World War II. I was trying to remember something else about him, but it didn't come through to me just then.

The two men had a brief conversation. Whitey was smiling and briefly clapped one hand on the other man's shoulder. Then the man in the cammies turned and came back down the stairs.

It didn't seem to me that Allison would be held in a home where they were staging a big party. Even with three stories, I didn't think anybody would take that kind of chance. And maybe the man in the cammies with the truck would now be driving to wherever Allison was being held. But I didn't know that for sure. I had an awful time making up my mind about what to do.

And then I decided. Whitey had to be my main man. If Allison wasn't in the house, he must know where she was being held. I watched the man in the cammies climb into the cab of the truck. He started the motor. My stomach flopped over. He drove off.

I sat down to rest my back against the side of the tree away from the house. Okay, Bragg, now what? They've got your girl and the man in the house probably knows where they've got her. But you're not the Invisible Man. You can't walk in and grab him by the scruff of the neck and drag him on out of there. He's having a party. People and drinking and laughing and flirting in the corners. You've got to get him out. How?

I tried to put myself in Whitey Whiteman's shoes. What is something that would force me to leave my own party, outside of somebody setting fire to the place? If I am him, I have killed, or arranged to have killed, three people to keep a secret. I smiled. The secret was my answer. CA 35. The tape.

I got to my feet with what I suspected was a mean grin on my face. I didn't have the tape, but I knew how to get him out of the house and away from the party. I jogged on up the road. I passed an angled extension of Lighthouse Avenue that ran on down to the ocean, a couple of hundred yards away. There was a navy reserve training center down that road, and at this time of night the road was dark and secluded. Considering what was behind all of this business, it seemed apt that there should be a navy facility there. I continued on up to where Asilomar intersected with the main part of Lighthouse that ran east through Pacific Grove. There was a motel at the intersection with an outside pay phone.

I dialed the motel Collins was at. Or was supposed to be at. He didn't answer the room phone.

"This is an emergency," I told the man at the desk. "Could you or somebody else run up to the room and knock on his door. Maybe he fell asleep."

We argued over it for a moment or two, but I convinced him it was important. He left the switchboard and made a quick trip up to the room. He was back a couple of minutes later, short of breath.

"Nobody there. At least they aren't answering any knocking on the door."

I thanked him and hung up. I thought about it. Maybe Collins had tried ringing me at Jo Sommers' home, and not getting me, drove over there himself. I dialed the Sommers number. No answer. I couldn't worry any longer about what might have happened to Collins. I looked up Whiteman's number in the directory and dialed it. After a while a woman's voice answered, with party noise roaring in the background. I asked for Whiteman, then waited some more. When

he came on the line I used a mock Chinese singsong
voice that a bad comic might use.

"Ho ho, hello, please. I have tape recording, you
catch 'em? Talky talk allabout CA thirty-five, ha-ha,
sailor boys all drown, you bet. X-ray Victor Mike
Love, we been hit by two torpedoes, you bet, but you
on secret mission, gotta go 'way chop-chop. Leave
poor sailor boys, many days out bake and float and
drown, you bet..."

"Who is this!" he demanded. He yelled it at the
top of his lungs, and some of the party noise in the
background quieted.

"You wanna leave party now, and come talk chop-
chop, or I send tape all 'round crazy place—lemme
see now, *Mon'rey Herald*, Gussy Wakefield, U.S. Navy
men, you bet. You come alone now, right now. You
drive down sailor reserve center on Lighthouse and
you keep lips tight about where you going. You come
down near gate, park long side road and get out car
and wait round, or you sure be sorry, Mr. CA thirty-
five man. Chop-chop."

I hung up the phone. If that didn't work I'd go
bust up the party. What the hell. I had two guns and
my pockets full of bullets, and somebody had my
girl. I left the phone and jogged on down the extension of Lighthouse and settled down in some shadows across the road from the entrance to the reserve
center gate. I didn't have long to wait. Headlights
swung around the corner of Asilomar, and a late-
model Cadillac tooled down the road and came to a
stop across the way. The driver doused the lights,
then shut off the motor and got out, staring in at the
dark navy building. I came up behind him with the
.38 in my hand.

"Put your hands on the roof of the car," I told
him.

He made a little start and glanced over his shoulder. "You!"

"Me. Hands on the roof of the car."

He did what I told him. He'd put on a dark sports jacket that hung oddly. "Leave your hands flat on the car roof and move back your feet about six inches." He moved his feet back. I holstered the .38 and was about to pat the pockets of the sports jacket when he tried to put a move on me.

He had a good little compact body and moved quickly. He pushed off from the car roof, ducked and whirled, his hand going for the right-hand jacket pocket. I gave him an open-handed clout along one ear and he crumpled onto the road. I reached down and took a .22-caliber revolver out of his jacket. I rolled him over and went over the rest of him without finding any other weapons. I opened the car door. He'd left the keys in the ignition. He was still stunned. I reached across and unlocked the passenger side door, then picked him up and shoved him headfirst across the seat of the car. I went around to the other side and wrestled him into the position I wanted him in, with his head down on the floor and his knees on the seat. I shut the door and went back and got behind the wheel. I wanted to get out of the immediate vicinity. I started the car and drove on down to the road that ran above the beach. I turned south and drove on a ways, then swung off onto a street that retreated from the ocean and did some winding around until I was sure nobody was trying to find us. I turned off onto a quiet, residential street and stopped the car. He was fully conscious again but not saying anything. I found a handkerchief in one of his pants pockets and tied it to the end of my own and used them to bind his hands behind his back. Then I went around to the passenger side again and pulled him out and sat him up on the seat. I got back in the car beside him. We could barely make out each other's face.

"Where's my girl?"

He didn't say anything. I cuffed him alongside the ear where I'd whacked him before.

"Where's my girl?"

"Why did you come back? We aren't going to hurt her. We just needed time..."

He stopped talking when I banged his ear again.

"Where's my girl?"

He sobbed, then said something so low I couldn't hear it.

"Speak up, before I make mush of your ear."

"I said she's down the coast."

"Is that where the man in the truck is headed for?"

He didn't answer right away. In fact he took altogether too long for the mood I was in right then. I made a fist this time and drove knuckles into his ear.

"Jesus, don't do that..."

"Is that where the man in the truck is headed for?"

"Yes! Don't hit me again. I can't hear."

I started the motor and got back onto a street that would take me out the back door of Pacific Grove and over to Highway 1, and turned south.

"What did you need time for?"

"To destroy the tapes. To find the Sommers woman."

"To kill her?"

He didn't reply right away. I took a hand away from the steering wheel and pulled it back to swing at him again.

"Yes!" he cried. "If it came to that. I had to end it."

"It's ended," I told him. "For you. How did your man know where to find the tapes at the Sommers home?"

"I've been there several times. He even pointed them out to me one time. The doctor did."

"Did he show you the ones he kept in a chest in his study as well? The ones to do with people living around here?"

He shook his head and looked as if he might be sick.

"How many men are with my girl?"

"Two. I mean one, right now. I hired two men. One's at the cabin. The man in the truck is going back there. He isn't as experienced. He's to relieve the man at the cabin. Then the man at the cabin— Dancer—is to find Mrs. Sommers."

"Was to find Mrs. Sommers. Get it through your head. It's all over with. Mrs. Sommers is stashed away and has men guarding her. Who killed Alex Kilduff?"

He made a sigh. "Dancer, and the other man."

"Why didn't they just shoot him and let it go at that? Why hang him from the flagpole?"

"He was a traitor. It was to warn off the rest of you."

"The rest of us weren't a part of it. Why was Alex Kilduff a traitor?"

"His father was aboard my ship, during the war."

"A radioman?"

"That's right. A radioman."

"And he was on duty when you heard the SOS from the *Indianapolis*."

"Yes. I assume he told Alex about that. And the boy must have had blackmail in mind for a very long time. I know others in the community were being blackmailed the same way. But only for piddling amounts of money. A thousand dollars. Two thousand. But it was just to set me up."

"How much money did he want from you?"

"A quarter million dollars. Two hundred and fifty thousand. It would break me."

"Who killed Dr. Sommers?"

He glanced across at me and hesitated, but not long enough for me to have to take one hand off the steering wheel again. "That was a mistake," he told me. "I thought he was the one behind the blackmail."

"Who killed him?"

He looked away. "Dancer did. But then I got another phone call." He fell silent.

"The girl in Big Sur. Who killed her?"

"Dancer again. I know somebody else who received a threat over the weekend, after Sommers was already dead. He was told to leave money with her. She had to be a part of it. And I meant to end it. I couldn't afford the money. I had a good career in the navy. I've been a successful man since. I just made one mistake, a long time ago. I couldn't let that become known. My home and family . . . My reputation and those of a lot of other good men were being threatened."

When I snorted he looked at me sharply. "Reputations," I muttered. "How far down the coast is this cabin?"

"Twenty miles, or thereabouts."

Once past Rio Road I opened up the big car. It was a little soft on the curves, but on the straightaway it hummed right up to 85 without a wheeze. It could have done more, but I wasn't used to driving that fast.

We swooshed across the bridge where the man in the cammies had dumped the cartons of tapes. "This is where your man disposed of the cassettes he took from the Sommers home. If he was coming back south later, why did he drive all the way back to your place? Why not just phone you?"

"I don't know the man that well. I've just been

taking things a step at a time. I didn't know I'd be sending him to relieve Dancer until he came by the house. How do you know where he disposed of the tapes?"

"I was a passenger on the truck. He just wasn't bright enough to know it."

Whiteman looked at the glow of the dashboard lights. "Maybe it *is* all over with," he said quietly.

"Believe it."

We strutted right along. I passed a couple of late-night travelers. A couple of miles further along I came up on the rear of the truck the man in cammies was driving.

"Get your head down," I told Whiteman.

He ducked down and I went on around the truck. I hadn't wanted to just ease back from him. He would have seen me coming up on him at high speed. If I fell back he might have become suspicious. A mile further along there was a wide turnout where people could pull off the road and gawk at the ocean below. It was a bright, moonlit night. I pulled off the road and parked and gawked at the water until the truck went past. I waited a couple of minutes more then fell in a good half mile behind him.

"Where'd Dancer come from?" I asked Whiteman.

"He's a merc."

"A what?"

"A mercenary. He does—all sorts of things, for a price. I didn't have connections with any gangland figures I could resort to for what had to be done. I had a discreet conversation with a friend. He told me about Dancer."

"What about the other man?"

"I don't know. He's somebody Dancer brought aboard last night."

"To help with Alex?"

"To help with—somebody was with the Sommers woman last night when he went to..." He looked away, out the window. "When he tried to dispose of her. I suppose it was you with her. Whoever it was chased Dancer. He said he got down on the beach and was well away from them, but then he took small-arms fire. Whoever it was came awful close to hitting him. He said anybody who could shoot that good with a handgun from that distance commanded respect. He wanted to call in this other man. I never even heard his name. But he lived just an hour or two away, up in Gilroy. They apparently got together later last night. By that time, through some phone calls I made, I learned that my old radioman, Kilduff, had a son now living in this area, and that it was Alex. I knew Alex, and I knew people who in turn knew where he lived. So I sent the men off to take care of the young man who had decided to use one of the navy's greatest wartime tragedies as part of a blackmail scheme. Such a man is beyond contempt."

I had no answer to that.

Chapter 20 ──────────────

We continued to wend our way south. Me and Whiteman in the Caddie and the guy in the truck. The feeling I was getting closer to Allison put me in a funny frame of mind. I even developed a fondness for the truck up ahead of me. It wasn't a speed demon, but it soldiered along doing its job. Up hill and down. Round the bend, over the bridge, climb the hill, flirt with the cliff. I wondered for a minute about the man in the truck. I even wondered if he had a wife and kids. Little chance of that, I thought, considering the sort of work he was doing. And just as well, I decided. Chances were about fifty-fifty he'd be dead before the night was over with.

We kept on trucking.

The man ahead of me turned off, finally, onto one of those roads you're apt to wonder about when you're idly driving down the coast. It was cut into the side of a small river valley coming down out of the hills to the east. It was an old dirt road, and there was a sign at the start of it I'd seen at other times. It warned that in rainy weather, the road wouldn't always be passable. It used to trigger my imagination. It made me think of mud and earth slides and old coots and bears burrowed down up in the hills somewhere for the winter.

When I turned onto the dirt road, I switched off

the headlights, using moonlight and a lot of concentration to move up closer behind the taillights of the truck. It was a road of ruts and warps and potholes. The Caddie had a better suspension system than the truck did. I moved up to within 100 yards of the other vehicle. A mile back into the hills, he turned off onto another road, in just as bad shape as the first. We went another half mile, part hilly, part flat. His destination was a moonlit meadow with the sound of running water off to one side. I stopped just shy of the clearing. The truck jounced on across toward a cabin at the far end with smoke coming out of a chimney. Another building that looked like a storage shed was a dozen paces to the left of the cabin.

I backed up a few yards, then swung the Cadillac around so it blocked the road, in the event anybody tried to drive back out. "That your cabin?" I asked Whiteman.

"Yes."

"What's the floor plan inside?"

He just looked at me a moment. "No. I suspect you are about to ruin the entire rest of my life. You'll have no more help from me, sir."

"Okay." I took out the .45 and gave him a sharp crack alongside the head. I didn't want him conscious and thinking slick thoughts while I was out there doing what I had to do.

I left the car and crept down one side of the meadow. The man ahead of me had swung the truck around in a circle so it was pointed back toward the road. The cabin door opened and another man stepped outside. I could see him clearly in the pool of light from the cabin. He also wore cammies. What a foolish way to go about life, I thought. He was bigger and older-looking than the truck driver. He had a grizzled look about him. They talked for a moment, and the bigger man gestured toward the inside of the cabin a time or two. The light they stood in had a flickering quality to it, and I realized the cabin didn't have electricity. The light must have come from a stove or fireplace and oil lamps. The two of them continued talking for several more moments. The bigger men even pulled the door behind him nearly closed. It was as if they didn't want somebody else inside to hear their conversation. Allison.

When they finally went inside I moved on around to the back to stand in the trees at the edge of the meadow. Moonlight reflected off a rear windowpane, but the room inside was dark. So it meant the structure was divided into at least two rooms. I moved up closer. The cabin's outer walls were made of rough-cut siding, as if somebody had set up a portable band saw and cut his own timber from the surrounding forest.

I stood staring at the rear window. I was sorely tempted to sneak up for a quick look inside, but there were too many things wrong with that idea. One of the men might enter the back room while I had my nose up against the window. I'd lose my one big edge, surprise. And if Allison was inside and saw me, whether she recognized me or not, she might let out a startled yelp and accomplish the same thing. An owl hooted a couple of times from nearby trees, agreeing with me.

But there was something else that I wanted to learn about the window itself. Crouching, I moved up on the cabin and squatted just beneath the pane of glass. It didn't look like a window that would open. They probably used it for light, not ventilation. I ducked back to the edge of the woods and continued on around to the other side of the cabin. That side had another window it it, with light coming through it. I made my way slowly on toward the shed, but I was still staring at the cabin window when

I should have had my eyes on the ground in front of me. I tripped over a root and fell hard, strangling a yelp in my throat and barking one fist when it hit the base of a tree trunk. At least it kept me from braining myself. I rolled and squatted for a moment, letting the pain subside and my breathing grow regular again. I dug out my penlight and used it briefly to continue on through the timber and out around to the side of the shed away from the cabin. I rested a minute, then peeked around the corner. The shed door faced the cabin. The door was equipped with a metal hasp and hoop. An old bolt was dropped through the hoop to keep the door closed. I lifted out the bolt, slid off the hasp and slowly opened the door. It squeaked a little, but not enough to alert the men in the cabin. I stepped inside and pulled shut the door behind me.

I dinked around the flash from the penlight. It was your average utility shed crammed with junk. Some tools and hardware, nails and bolts and a couple of rolls of wire. Sandpaper and paint and stiff brushes. Some scrap plywood was stacked against one end. I didn't see any rope, which I'd been hoping to find, but decided one of the rolls of wire would do as well. It was about the thickness of the piece of hard graphite in a lead pencil. I found a pair of wire cutters among the tools, snipped off a piece of the wire and used that to fasten the rest of the coil to my belt. I tucked the wire cutters into a hip pocket, put my penlight away and swung open the shed door just enough for me to peek around its edge and scan the cabin. Things seemed calm enough. I stepped outside, put the bolt back across the hasp and retreated around behind the shed to where I couldn't be seen from the cabin. I took the .45 out of its shoulder holster and jacked a round into the chamber. I took out the .38 and cocked the hammer.

I carried the .45 in my right hand, the .38 in my left. I left the shed and trotted across the clearing to the other side of the cabin, so that if anybody opened the cabin door, I'd be shielded from sight behind it. I didn't consciously think about these things. My body just did them. With the tension and adrenaline shooting through me the way they were just then, thinking would have been a handicap.

I came up on the cabin and stopped a step away from the door. It was fitted with a hasp and locking hoop similar to those on the shed. The door also had a little thumb latch fitted through the door. I clicked the latch, threw open the door and stepped inside.

The bigger of the two men was sitting in a chair tilted back against the right rear wall, near a doorway leading into the back room of the cabin. His buddy was standing along the opposite wall fixing himself a sandwich from a platter of cold cuts on a table near the window. A lamp was on the food table, another was on a stand beside the fellow tilted back in the chair and now lowering a magazine he'd been looking through.

There was a Franklin stove with a dying fire in it halfway along the wall where the fellow was sitting. There were two more chairs and a couple of sleeping bags along the wall to my left.

"Just freeze," I told them.

The fellow making the sandwich looked as if his heart had jumped up into his throat. The older man lowered himself slowly until his chair was back on the floor. He put up his hands and got to his feet.

"Well, well, well, well," he said softly, with a voice that reminded me of rural Texas. "Two-gun Gus, come to call." He said it with a smile and a glance across the room to his partner.

Maybe they had talked over what they'd do in a situation like that. The instant their eyes met they moved. The man to my right smashed his magazine into the light beside him, while his partner knocked over the lamp on the table. Then the bigger man went through the door behind him and his buddy went through the window next to him headfirst. I fired the .38 after the man going out the window. I didn't fire toward the back room. I crunched on glass, crossing to the shattered window. The man was up and running a zigzag pattern toward the woods. I sent a round from the .45 after him, not expecting to hit him, just to keep him moving away.

I crossed back to the inner door. I'd heard the man who went through it slide a bolt across it from inside. That was fine. It was where I wanted him for now. I pulled off the loop of wire and in the glow of light still coming from the stove, snipped off a long piece of it and coiled it several times around the doorknob. I dragged over the table with the cold cuts on it and positioned it across the doorway. It filled it and then some. I made several loops of wire from the doorknob to one table leg. To get out now, the man inside would either have to go through the back window or pull the table through the walls. I didn't think he was ready to go through the window yet. Allison, if she was in there, was supposed to be his ace in the hole.

I took a quick look out at the meadow from the cabin doorway, then ran out and over to the tree line on the opposite side of the meadow from where the man had gone through the window. I went back up the side of the meadow, then crossed over until I had the truck between me and the cabin. I trotted up behind the truck and crawled in under it. I'd tucked the .38 back into the belt holster. Now I took it out, removed the shell casing of the one round I'd fired from it and replaced it with another cartridge from the box in my pocket. I reholstered it, then waited with the .45 out and ready.

The man who'd gone through the window came out of the shadows about ten minutes later. He'd been doing a circuit of the meadow, the same as I had. He came out of the woods on my left and dashed around to behind the cabin. I could hear him speaking. He was talking through the closed window, to the man inside. The older man would be telling his partner to go around into the cabin and undo whatever I'd done to seal off the rear room. A moment later the outside man came into view. He was crouched low, and stayed still that way, studying the territory. I had the automatic in a two-handed grip, braced against one of the truck wheels. When the man in cammies rose to a semi-crouch and started to round the corner of the cabin, I fired off two rounds, aiming for the lower part of his body.

The big slugs slammed him against the corner of the cabin as if he'd been hit by a bull. He gave a startled yelp, then his body fell to the ground.

"Your head is directly in my line of sight," I yelled to him. "Throw away any weapon you have and move your hands away from your body."

His hands jerked out from his sides. "Lost my gun when I was hit," he called.

"Stay frozen or the next round goes through your skull," I yelled. I got out from beneath the truck and trotted down to him. He was in pain. There was blood soaking one trouser leg just above his knee.

"You got a bone," he told me. "Leg's paralyzed. I can't move."

"Save your breath," I told him. "I'm going to move you." I put away the automatic and took him under the arms and dragged him back toward the truck. When I got him there I put his hands behind his back and wired them together. He winced in pain but didn't say anything.

I left him propped against a wheel of the truck and ran down to the shed. I prayed I had time before the other man decided to go out the back window. It would have been the smart thing for him to do right then, but he'd be abandoning the hostage I expected was back there with him.

In the shed I grabbed one of the pieces of scrap plywood, some sixteen-penny nails and a hammer. I pounded a nail part of the way into each of the corners, then lugged the plywood down to the cabin. I sneaked a peek around a back corner. The pane of glass was intact. I scuttled over in a crouch and slid the board up over the window and pounded in the two bottom nails. I heard a noise from inside when I stood along one side of the board and pounded in one of the top nails, ducked down under the window and hammered in the other.

"Hey! What the hell's going on out there?" yelled a muffled voice. Then he made a mistake. He tried to shoot through the plywood. He did make a nick in it, but he also shattered the pane of glass inside. He made a yelp.

I had once told Allison that if she ever got into trouble, she could know that I'd be coming after her. And once she knew I was in the vicinity, she was to tuck herself into as small a ball as she could in a corner and just sit tight. I hoped that was what she was doing just then, and that the flying glass hadn't cut her. There are chances that have to be taken in the sort of work that I do.

I hammered in more nails, sealing off the only exit the man inside had right then.

"I've got the girl," he shouted when I'd finished hammering. "You goddamn fool! Don't you know I have the girl?"

I didn't say a word. I just took the hammer and the rest of the nails back to the shed. I used my penlight to look around for other things. I found just the ticket, a couple of sturdy eyehooks. I took a nail and the hammer and a screwdriver back inside the cabin. I used the hammer and nail to start a hole into a bottom corner of the door and the door frame opposite. Then I used the screwdriver as a lever through the loops of the eyehooks to screw them in where I'd started the holes. I figured that somewhere down the line the man in back would think to take apart the doorknob inside in an attempt to loosen what was holding him in there. It didn't matter, once I'd used another length of wire to connect the two eyehooks.

These fellows in their cammies offering their guns for hire would know about things like T-ambushes, wind drift and long-range rifle fire, and maybe a boobie trap or two.

I knew about close-in fire, street work and fear. They also would know about fear, from artillery and air assault. But I knew about fear of another sort. I went back over to the man beside the truck. He wasn't exactly alert, but he was conscious. I squatted down beside him.

"Whether you live or die this night—whether or not you will ever be able to walk on that leg again—is all going to depend on the next five minutes," I told him. "You are holding a blonde woman hostage in the rear of the cabin, correct?"

"Yes, sir. But we haven't hurt her none. She's a good hostage."

He had an edgy twang. He might have lived in Tennessee at one time.

"How is she restrained?"

"Tied with rope."

"Does she have a blindfold?"

"Yes, sir. As much for her own protection as ours."

In more ways than one, I thought. The blindfold would have helped protect her eyes when the other man tried to shoot through the plywood and sent glass flying.

"You and your partner killed a young man over in Monterey last night or early this morning, then hoisted him up a flagpole."

"I've never killed anybody in the States. I don't contract for that. But yes, I did help Dancer arrange the body after. It was a little eccentricity the man who's payin' us asked for."

"Earlier yesterday one of you killed a girl down in Big Sur."

"I don't know anything about that."

"One of you lobbed a grenade into the patio of a home up in Carmel Highlands last night, at the same house where you picked up the cartons of cassettes tonight."

"That was Dancer, sir. He got me down here right after that. He decided he wanted some help."

"Did Dancer smother a man at the same house Friday night?"

"No, sir. At least Dancer told me the man paying us did that himself. He hired Dancer after that. Dancer said he told the man—Whiteman—that if he wanted some killing done, that Dancer would have to be sure the man hiring him would back him a hundred percent. I guess by telling Dancer he'd already killed a man himself, he felt Dancer would trust him like that."

Either Dancer or Whiteman was lying. Each said the other had killed Sommers. I didn't think this man was lying. He was frightened and hurting. But I wasn't going to get sidetracked by who might be lying. Let others sort it out. I wanted Allison.

"Which pocket are the truck keys in?"

"The left."

I reached in and got them, then grabbed him under the arms again and dragged him off a little ways from the truck. Now was going to be the tricky part. Terrorize the man in the cabin without giving Allison a heart attack along with him.

I climbed up into the truck cab, turned over the motor and let her run for a minute, then drove around behind the cabin. I pointed the front of the truck toward the rear of the meadow. The steel-rimmed truck bed faced the back of the cabin. I put the truck in reverse, gunned the motor and backed into the rear of the cabin with a stunning jolt.

The man in the cabin began shouting. I drove forward a ways, put the truck in reverse and backed into the rear cabin wall again. I changed gears and drove around to the right side of the cabin. I aimed the truck bed at a portion of the wall that was more toward the front of the cabin, rather than near the back room where the man and Allison were. I really let them have it this time. The blows on the rear wall had been love taps compared with what I gave the side wall. It doubled me over the steering wheel when I bounced off the rear seat, and the motor stalled. I started her up again, drove forward, changed gears and slammed back into the cabin again. I heard something beginning to splinter.

I drove around to the other side of the cabin and took a couple of runs at the wall over there. I drove around back and made a couple more runs against the rear bedroom wall. Hard knocks, they were. Dancer was yelling again. He was beginning to sound hoarse. I drove around to the side without a window, lined up the truck bed once more, but then just sat there with the motor idling. I waited three minutes by my watch, letting Dancer wonder about what was going to happen next, then I put the truck in gear and gave the side wall another whack. It killed the motor again. Before I could start it again I heard a rapping noise from in back. I started the truck and drove off a little distance from the cabin. I left the motor idling and went around back to see what the noise was. Dancer had found something to try to loosen the plywood board over the window. He was getting one of the lower corners worked loose. When it started to give a little more he abandoned his tool and began to slam it with the heel of his hand. It was loosened enough so I could hear him a little better. He was making something between a honk and a grunt while he worked.

I walked over to the edge of the meadow and set myself up partly behind a tree. I was about thirty feet from the cabin. Dancer didn't bother removing all of the plywood. When he got both lower corners loose he worked on the sides until he could swing the board out from the bottom. Part of his head appeared below the plywood. He turned it, as if listening to the sound of the truck motor I'd left running, then he boosted himself headfirst out the window, letting the plywood hang loose behind him. He was still on the ground when I yelled at him.

"Freeze, Dancer! Make yourself spread-eagle!"

Fear clouded his judgment. He rolled, brought up a gun and fired wildly into the trees around me. I waited until he started to scramble to his feet, then shot at the thickest part of the target his body presented. It was no time for trick shooting. It was time for workmanship. I shot three times. He bucked and rolled, then just lay there with his knees tucked up toward his stomach. I moved out and came up on him from behind. A 9-millimeter automatic was on the ground nearby. I scooped it up, then knelt beside him, patting his body for concealed weapons. He had a knife strapped to his left shin. I unstrapped it and tossed it aside. He wasn't conscious any longer. Blood was making a big, damp patch at his waist. He probably had some big problems inside him. But they wouldn't be any bigger than the ones he'd dealt Alex Kilduff and Nikki Scarborough.

I got up, walked over to the cabin wall and lifted the plywood. I worked it the rest of the way free and tossed it aside.

"Hi ho, Bragg here," I said through the opening.

I got out the penlight and flashed it around inside the room. I'd been right. Dancer had slid back the bolt on the door and had tried to dismantle the doorknob. Allison was in the corner opposite the door, and it looked as if she'd remembered my advice. She was sitting on the floor with her back against the wall and her knees tucked up in front of her. Her hands were tied behind her back, but she'd worked loose a corner of the blindfold. They also had put a gag across her mouth. She was trying to say something through it.

"You look cute, even like that," I told her.

Her reply was muffled, but it sounded like a swear-word. Which was unusual for Allison.

"I'll be there in a minute," I told her.

I went around into the cabin and snipped through all the wiring I'd done. I shoved the table out of the way and opened the door. The doorknob came off in my hand. I went on in and cut through the rope around Allison's wrists. She started to massage them while I took off the gag and blindfold.

"Hi, babe," I told her.

"Hi," she said, then took a deep breath and leaned her head back against the wall. "Well," she said after another moment. "I certainly did learn what I wanted."

"What's that?"

"Whether I can live with the sort of violence you

encounter. Not only encounter, but dish out, even. I didn't know if you wanted to kill him or me."

"I was hoping you'd remember what I told you to do if something like this ever happened to you."

"I remembered. When they first took me—I'd gone to sketch the Stilwell home..."

"I know."

"Anyway, I wasn't so much frightened as I was just plain mad. They put a cloth over my face with some evil-smelling chemical that was supposed to knock me out, I guess. But it never did. They tied me and put a blindfold on and tossed me on the floor of a car and threw a blanket over me, then just drove around like I was a sack of potatoes or something. Then we went somewhere and I was put into a room by myself. About an hour later they trotted me out again and drove me somewhere to where I could speak to you on a phone, then they drove me down here. And by the time we got down here, it had all just sort of welled up inside of me. I began to call them every form of asshole under the sun. I mean, it was crazy. Me, Allison France, using that sort of language? But I heard myself doing it. Felt good. They had one very angry lady on their hands. That's when they gagged me. After that I just sat back here until I heard a different car or something drive up."

"Truck. I was following it."

"I guess. And then a little later I heard the front door bang open and you yell, 'Freeze!' like a G-man or something, and then all hell broke loose, but you know about that. By then I'd managed to use my shoulder to nudge up one side of the blindfold so I could watch some of the action. The man who came in here spent a lot of time looking out the window, trying to figure out what was happening. When he heard shooting he tried to go back out the door here. You must have done something to block it."

"I did."

"He was trying to figure out what to do about that when you put something up over the window and began to hammer it into place. I think he began to go to pieces about then. He tried to shoot out the window, but it didn't seem to work the way he thought it would. Some glass must have hit him in the face. I heard him cursing. I just tried to make myself small and hoped he'd forget about me. He had a flashlight he took out then and started working on the doorknob, then you began ramming the place with—what was that, a tank?"

"Just the truck."

"Well, just the truck was more than enough to make the man in here practically disintegrate before my eyes. He began using the flashlight finally to smash away at a corner of whatever you had over the window. But I guess you saw all that."

"Most of it."

"Then I heard more shooting. I guess you won, since you're here and he isn't."

"You got it."

"Where is he?"

"Outside. Bleeding to death, probably. I couldn't take any chances."

"Well," said Allison, with a little sigh. "I guess Mrs. France's daughter has really turned a corner."

"How's that?"

"There was a time the thought of a man maybe bleeding to death nearby would have completely unstrung me."

"Not now?"

"Nope. Not after this. In fact, he made me so mad I'm sorely tempted to ask for the loan of a gun so I can go plug him a couple of times myself."

Chapter 21 —————

The sorting out took a little bit of doing. The cabin had a first-aid kit, and I patched up the two wounded men as best I could. Dancer was still breathing, but that was the most you could say for him. I propped him into a corner of the truck cab where he could benefit from the heater, but that was my only concession. I was having Allison drive the Cadillac back out, and there was no way I was going to put one of her captors in there with her. I put the other wounded man into the bed of the truck, and after replacing the handkerchiefs binding Whiteman's hands with wire, I tossed him back there, too.

We got down out of the hills. At the first roadside pay phone we stopped and I got hold of Collins and Reinhardt at the motel in Monterey. As I'd suspected, Collins had been worried about me when he'd tried to phone me at the Sommers home. He'd apparently been traveling between the two places when I tried to phone him from near Whiteman's home. Another agency man had finally arrived to relieve Reinhardt in Salinas. I told them what had happened and we discussed what we should do next. They promised to put things into action.

By the time we got to the shopping center off Rio Road on the outskirts of Carmel, they had a couple of ambulances and some men from the sheriff's department waiting. The story I gave the law focused for the most part right then on Allison's kidnapping and my releasing her after a gunfight with the wounded men. Dancer and the other man were taken off to the hospital with a sheriff's deputy escort. I told the other investigators what Dancer had said about Whiteman's being the one who smothered Woody Sommers, and they said they'd get a search warrant and go through his closets looking for the clothing I remembered seeing him in earlier that night at the Hunt Club. Then their lab people would see what they could come up with.

I told them I'd be by to tell them more about it later, then Allison and I got a ride back to the motel in Monterey. I phoned Ceejay and let her talk with Allison, then we got cleaned up and slept for most of the rest of the day.

By the time we were up and feeling human again, Collins and Reinhardt had checked out and returned to San Francisco. They'd picked up my car at the airport in Watsonville and left it parked outside. I'd given them the key to the Sommers home, and they'd gone by and gotten the other tapes that were in the chest in the Sommers study. Then they called Jo and told her it was okay to go home again. I'd told them to pitch the tapes into the ocean somewhere on their way home.

Allison and I drove over to Carmel, ravenous. For me, there's always been a simple answer when I am ravenous. Allison agreed, so we went to London's and had a couple of their fancy cheeseburgers. Before we left there I made a couple of phone calls and arranged for a little meeting. The people I called were reluctant, but willing.

When Allison and I drove back out the Carmel Valley and climbed the road to Gus Wakefield's home, Jo Sommers was waiting in her own car at the bottom of the Wakefield driveway. I had told Jo on the phone about the ordeal Allison had been through, and Jo expressed the proper amount of dismay and sympathy.

Allison shrugged. "Except for the inconvenience," she told Jo, "it was a piece of cake."

Jo blinked at her, then turned toward me as we started up the driveway. "I really don't know about this, Peter. I'll feel terribly uncomfortable."

"How do you think General Wakefield felt when he heard his brother's voice on that tape? Come on, Jo, you owe him."

She made a little shudder, but continued on. Gus Wakefield answered the door himself and invited us into the big living room looking out over the Valley. If anybody else was home, they were keeping out of sight and hearing.

After he'd poured drinks for us all, I brought Gus up-to-date on what had been happening; and as best I could, I tried to explain Jo's foolish role in what all along had really been a scheme cooked up by Alex sometime after his father told him about the SOS from the *Indianapolis*. I didn't know if I believed her all that strongly myself, but the important thing was, these people all had to live with one another for the foreseeable future, and I wanted the people around there who'd been affected by it in one way or another to realize the thing was ended.

At first I hadn't planned to reveal Whiteman's role in the *Indianapolis* affair, but it occurred to me that Whiteman had money and that meant he'd have a pretty good lawyer, and who could say what punishment might be dealt out in a courtroom before it was all over with.

When I was through talking, I turned to Jo Sommers, and right on cue, she apologized for her part of it.

"I never, ever, could imagine that it would come to this," she said quietly, staring at her feet. "And I hope, Gus, you'll tell anybody who was touched by all this how ashamed I am. I understand from what Peter has told me that the tapes have all been destroyed. I hope they are. If I ever find any more of them, I'll destroy them myself. I mean that."

"I'm sure you do," said Wakefield, getting to his feet and pacing for a moment. "I just can't figure out what would possess Whitey..."

He sat back down and clasped his hands between his knees. "He should have gone to Woody Sommers and had it out with him. Not the way you said he did, of course. This whole thing might have been prevented. That's the great flaw you know, in many of us who've spent our lives in the service of our country. Some of us have never learned to come to grips with the passions and drives of other human beings, off the battlefield. West Point? The Naval Academy? They're engineering schools. We're pump fixers and mechanics and mathematicians. We're not social scientists. Sometimes we're just out of our element."

"Sometimes we all are," I suggested.

"Amen," said Allison, getting to her feet. "You know, Bragg, you've just hit it on the head. I've never felt so far out of my element in my life. Not that it hasn't been a thrill a minute, but would you mind taking me home, please?"

So I did that, in stages. First to the motel in Monterey, then the next day to my apartment in Sausalito, and the day after that, up the coast to her own home in Barracks Cove.

I kept in touch with the Monterey authorities. Dancer, it turned out, didn't make it. He was conscious at some point and made a statement to investigators, admitting the killing of Nikki Scarborough and Alex

Kilduff, at Whiteman's order. He died the following day. His buddy, whose name I never did learn, spent some time in the hospital, then a few days in Monterey County jail, but he was eventually released. Allison and I didn't feel it was worth our while to try tagging him with kidnapping charges.

The crime lab had been able to find some hairs they identified as coming from Woody Sommers on a jacket Whiteman wore the night Sommers was killed. The former destroyer skipper and his attorney were trying to plea-bargain their way through the legal thicket, but chances were he'd spend some time in prison.

And I spent the whole next week with Allison, reading while she was working out in her studio, taking walks on the beach with her, eating at restaurants or barbecuing things in her backyard. It was a way of getting our blood pressure back to normal.

Then one day when I phoned the office they told me I'd had a call from a Captain McDonnough with the San Francisco Police Department. My shoulders tensed when I heard that. McDonnough was the original hardcase, the only man I knew who had the capacity to make me quake in my boots. He was head of the police intelligence unit. And if he wanted to see me, I'd have to drive down and go on up to his office, right next door to that of the chief of police himself, and see what the captain wanted of me.

I told Allison all this later that evening, sitting on the floor in front of a fire in her small fireplace, sipping brandy. She accepted it with a nod of her head, then turned to me with a little frown.

"Gee, I almost forgot," she told me, making a fist and giving me a little punch on the shoulder.

"What's that?"

"Thanks for a helluva jazz festival."